I0682740

BLOODHOUND INVESTIGATIONS

A HOWARD PIERCE INVESTIGATES STORY

EVELYN INFANTE

Printed in the United States of America

ISBN #978-1-950625-21-5

Cover Design by Wesley Goulart

Publisher:

Shaggy Dog Productions
www.ShaggyDogProductions.online

To the real Sherlock Holmes detectives,
who see what others miss.

1

_____

$\mathcal{B}$ecause of flash flooding in the area, he ditched his habit of taking his usual route on the back roads and turned onto Route 80.

He thought that this storm will keep even the early risers in bed longer than usual. After the first clap of thunder made him jump, he nervously drove slowly despite wanting to get there as fast as possible. Rain fell on his windshield in buckets, and he clenched the steering wheel trying to focus his vision through rapidly moving wipers.

Twenty minutes past his usual drive time, he pulled into the Coral Bells Adult Living apartments' parking lot. He turned off the engine, reached for the umbrella with a trembling hand, and breathed deeply. _I can do this._

Wanting to get it done before he lost his nerve, he swung the car door open and clicked the umbrella's automatic button as he stepped out of the car and into a puddle of water rushing across the blacktop.

"Fuck me!" he yelled into the storm and slammed the door shut. He'd forgotten to put on his rubber boots.

Sloshing his way around to the passenger side, he pulled

open the door and picked up the double plastic bags protecting a box of day-old baked goods he brought home from work last night. He intended to give the confections to his neighbor as a treat for his three children, but the neighbor declined his offer. His children ate too much sugar and were being weaned off sweets.

Why didn't I throw these damn donuts into the trash?

Hands full, he pushed the door shut with his hip and pressed the key fob button already in hand, careful not to tip the box or crush the doughnuts. Thunder rumbled all around him and seconds later, the sky lit up with flashes of lightning. "Oh shit," he muttered.

The wind whipped and raged, doing its best to turn the umbrella inside out as he hurried, hoping he didn't get struck by lightning. With less than a few yards to get from the parking lot to the front of the building, he struggled, having one hell of a time fighting the wind and sideways rain which pelted his face as he sprinted to the front door—one hand gripping the umbrella for dear life as the other tried to protect the package.

Somewhat weatherworn, he made it to the entrance. With a chilled index finger, he pushed the button. After identifying himself to the voice on the intercom, the buzzer sounded, and he pushed the door open with his shoulder.

Josephine Devin, the security guard on duty, took her eyes off her magazine and stared as he gently put his package on the floor and pulled a conical plastic bag from its holder. She almost laughed out loud when he tried to shove his dripping umbrella inside the plastic, failing every time he tried spreading the plastic apart with the tip of the umbrella. Grumbling, he finally succeeded and shot her an embarrassed smile.

Tempering his annoyance, he grabbed his package off the floor. Shoes squishing and water dripping from his pant legs and raincoat forming small puddles with every step, he trudged his way toward the front desk. "Good morning," he greeted, with an enthusiasm he did not feel.

Josephine looked past him to the wet floor and pointed her chin. "Better find a mop and dry that up before someone slips and gets hurt," she admonished.

He turned his head and stared at the floor. "I'll get some paper towels. It's too early to go searching for a mop," he said, hoping to get away.

"What are you doing here so early?" she scoffed. "On a day like today, I'd be curled up in my bed until the last minute before *I* had to get up."

He had anticipated the question and thought it best to keep it simple. "Storm woke me, and I couldn't get back to sleep, so I thought I'd come in instead of lying awake in my bed."

"Really? I love a downpour like this. All that thunder and lightning would've kept *me* asleep for hours. You should've stayed in bed. You look like a wet puppy," she smirked. "How bad is it out there, anyway?"

"Pretty bad," he said in no mood for chitchat.

Reaching for the box of tissues on her desk, Josephine said, "Wipe your face." She opened a drawer and took out a sheet of paper when he snatched the box from her hand.

He quickly dabbed his face, desperate to get past her. "Thank you."

"Sign in please," she said.

He grabbed one of many pens in a holder and scratched his name on the timesheet, dropping the pen on the desk. Josephine picked it up and initialed the time next to his name. She then held out her open hand.

"What? he said.

"The tissues."

He gave her the wet tissues he held tightly in his fist, but she eyed his package before he could take two steps.

"What you got there?"

"Day-old donuts," he said, trying again to move past.

Josephine's eyes lit up. "Ooh, can I have one?"

Fuck! I Shoulda said it was a bag full of moldy cheese.

With a taut smile, he said, "Sure," placing the package on her desk, "help yourself."

She pulled the box out of the bags and wheeling her chair to the basket she threw away the wet tissues and plastic bags. She then rolled back, pulled the box closer, and flipped the lid open. "Oh, my," she said, eyes growing big with anticipation.

"Best choose your favorite before I take them into the coffee room."

"They all look so yummy," she said with delight. She then waved her hand over the box as if caressing each delectable-looking pastry.

Whenever he thought she was about to take one, she drew her hand back, wiggled her fingers, and resumed scrutinizing the tantalizing assortment. It took all he had not to scream, 'pick one already.' Instead, he clenched and unclenched his fists, holding on to a counterfeit smile, while water dripped from his hair down his neck and back, making him shiver. Before he could suppress it, a monstrous-sounding sneeze shot out of his nostrils and gaping mouth, barely giving him time to turn his head away from her desk and cover his face.

Josephine's head snapped up. "Wow, that's quite a sneeze. Bless you." She again reached for the box of tissues, offered it to him, and turned her attention back to the donuts.

"Thank you." He anxiously pulled out a couple of tissues and blew his nose. It took all of his self-control not to snatch the box of pastries and run. Instead, he walked around her desk and tossed the used tissues in the wastebasket, trying to control his impatience.

Finally, without taking her eyes off the donuts, Josephine plucked a tissue out of the box and gingerly lifted out a coconut custard. She then pulled out an extra to fold around the doughnut. Opening a desk drawer, she reached for her oversized purse and deposited her snack in it. All the while, he stared at her little show, doing his best to hide his mounting frustration.

"Thank you. I'll take this goody home with me." Josephine looked at her watch. "Less than two hours before my shift's over."

He reached for the box, closed the lid, and picked it up, still smiling. "Enjoy."

Me and my fucking habit of not wasting food.

He dropped his fake smile as soon as he had his back to her, and almost ran to the empty coffee room, where he threw the bakery box onto a table near the coffeemaker.

The clock on the wall read 6:13 a.m.

Damn. Gotta hurry.

Thanks to Josephine's theatrical indecision, he had no time to change out of his wet clothes and shoes.

Josephine wandered into the coffee room to look for him when he didn't return. Not finding him there, she opened the cupboard and found a roll of paper towels. Annoyed, she went back to the foyer and bent down to wipe up his mess.

fter his wife's death, Wane Rudolph stopped caring about himself and least of all, the condition of his house. Along with doubling down on sweets, he began eating whatever microwaveable, processed food he could find in the supermarket freezer. Three months after his wife's passing, he had added an extra twenty-five pounds to his bulk. He'd always struggled with his weight, but his wife, Lilly had kept a watchful eye on his eating habits. She knew he'd sometimes sneak a sweet or a burger with fries when he went out, but chose not to confront him for his weakness.

Newly married, Wane would often quote the old catchphrase to his wife, 'cleanliness is next to godliness,' when he found dishes in the sink fifteen minutes after breakfast, or he thought the house needed vacuuming or dusting.

Lilly would calmly explain, "I didn't forget the dishes, dear. They're soaking. I'll get to them after I make the bed," or she would say, "I will tend to the housework. Don't you worry about it."

But his nitpicking continued whenever he thought she had failed in her duties as the woman of the house. Eventually,

Wane took on Lilly's role as a housekeeper, convinced he'd do a better job. Lilly readily agreed with his decision, relieved he stopped hounding her about cleanliness and godliness.

With more time to indulge in her passion for cooking, their meals became gourmet worthy. They both took turns with the laundry, and they did the marketing together. It was an arrangement that worked for them.

Alas, as sometimes happens in marriage, theirs hadn't always been the picture of an idyllic union. Wane was devoutly religious. His wife, while also religious, was not fanatical, as she believed her husband to be.

Once their son was born, Wane took it upon himself to educate Lilly about the importance of a man's role as head of the family, and his wife and children as subordinates.

They were both relaxing in the living room one evening after dinner. She read the latest detective novel, while Wane scrutinized his bible as usual. Turning to one of many dog-eared pages, he leaned forward and said, "Lilly, listen to this. It says right here, '... the husband is the head of the wife.'" Wane turned to another page. "And here it says, '... no woman to teach or have authority over a man, rather she is to remain silent.'" He stared at Lilly through his reading glasses expecting her to agree.

Lilly was smart enough to know anything she said to contradict what he believed would end in an argument. Instead, she listened respectfully, slightly bowed her head, and returned to her reading. Wane took her nod as acquiescence.

But everyone has their limit. One evening when Wane began his usual lecture, Lilly reached hers. Perhaps because he constantly interrupted her reading as she put together clues to the mystery, or she'd grown weary of her husband's constant bible rants, she reacted.

"Wane," she said, with a voice louder than she customarily used. The surprised look on his face gave her pause. Gritting her teeth and taking a deep breath to control her anger, she said, "I will not obey you like a sheep, and kowtow as an inferior no matter what it says in your bible. Please stop quoting those old verses to me. They're just stories."

Wane sprung from his recliner like a cat after his prey and repaid his wife's audacity with a slap. "This is the Word of God," he yelled. "How dare you disrespect our Lord?"

Lilly dropped her book and ran into their bedroom, locking the door behind her. Wane went after her and banged on the bedroom door. "Come out here, Lilly. I'm trying to teach you something."

When she didn't answer, he put his ear to the door. Hearing her sobs, he walked away, thinking she would come to her senses and apologize. After a while, he regretted striking her. He gently rapped on the bedroom door. "I'm sorry, Lilly. Please come out. I promise never to lay my hands on you again."

When she calmed down, Lilly opened the door and rushed into his arms, forgiving him.

But bullies don't give up control over others so easily, and the pattern of abuse increased over the years.

After their son died, her only reason for putting up with Wane's flare-ups, Lilly left Wane and went to live with her parents.

He called her every day. "Please come home," he begged, "I need you."

Lilly couldn't bear the pain she heard in his voice when he pleaded with her. They had lost their only son, and she needed to be comforted by her husband as much as he needed her solace. But she wouldn't come home unless he agreed to get counseling. She adamantly told him, "I will not let you bully me ever again, Wane. I refuse to live with a violent man."

"I promise. I'll do anything you say," he immediately agreed.

Wane began seeing a counselor for his anger issues, never

missing an appointment. After a few weeks, Lilly came home to care for her inconsolable husband.

Although he still regularly read his bible, he never again used its parables as a weapon to dominate his wife. They transitioned into a comfortable and loving existence for the remainder of her life.

After Lilly's funeral, Wane made it clear he did not want visitors or condolence phone calls. He told everyone, "Please don't trouble yourselves cooking for me. I have plenty of food in the freezer, and at a time like this, I prefer to be alone."

At first, people did not believe him, theorizing it was his grief talking. They would ring his doorbell laden with casseroles and offers of companionship but left feeling insulted and unappreciated despite their sympathy for his loss.

Tired of repeating himself, Wane turned up the volume on his television set if someone came calling, whether it be a neighbor, fellow parishioner, or the pastor of his church. Their commiseration reminded Wane of the guilt he felt for sleeping through Lilly's hour of need. He closed himself off from human contact, punishing himself for his wife's death.

Word got around Wane wasn't answering the door. Some took to telephoning him at all hours, inquiring about his wellbeing. He'd cut them off, repeating he was fine but wanted to be left alone. The neighborhood finally got the message, leaving him to wallow in his misery.

———

IN 1985, Jenaro Miller and his wife, Carmen, moved next door to the Rudolphs. They soon became close friends. When Lilly Rudolph died in 2005, it had been four years since Jenaro's wife died of breast cancer. He understood well a husband's grief for his loving wife and called to check on his friend the day after the funeral, gently offering help with anything he needed. Wane rejected every attempt Jenaro made to help him get through his sorrow.

"Please leave me alone," Wane told Jenaro the last time he telephoned.

Jenaro let him be for a few weeks but sick with worry, he tired of waiting for an invitation and got in his car for the two-hour drive to Wane's home. He felt their long friendship had given him the right to ignore Wane's wishes.

Determined to get inside, Jenaro firmly knocked on Wane's door.

"Go away." came an angry voice from within the house.

"Wane, open the door. It's me, Jenaro."

"I told you, I want to be left alone," Wane screeched.

Undeterred, Jenaro warned, "You better open the door because I'm not leaving."

When he didn't hear a reply, he knocked harder. A neighbor opened his door. "Hey, what's all that racket going on?"

Jenaro said, "I apologize for the noise, but I need to check on my friend."

"Oh, yes, Wane," said the neighbor. "Haven't seen him since the funeral. The last time I knocked, he didn't open the door for me either. Doesn't want company, but you go ahead and see if he lets you in."

"Jenaro said, thank you," and the neighbor nodded and went back into his apartment.

He now banged louder on Wane's door and didn't stop until Wane yanked the door open.

"Go home and leave me alone," Wane said irritably.

Jenaro's heart skipped a beat. Wane appeared bloated with the extra weight he had put on. He had dark circles underneath his eyes, and his unshaven face looked blotchy. Jenaro averted his gaze, trying to ignore the stained pajamas.

"Too bad. I'm coming in," he said. He pushed Wane out of the way and barged straight into the living room where he stopped cold, stunned at the piles of dirty dishes, strewn candy wrappers, empty beer bottles, and pizza boxes on the coffee table.

He gave Wane a what-the-hell-look.

"Mind your own business," Wane said, looking away in apparent shame.

"No," Jenaro said. "I will not mind my business. You need help."

"I don't need any help," Wane insisted, anger rising.

"We'll see about that after we've cleaned up this place and you've had a shower and a shave. You look like shit."

Wane glared at his old friend, intent on standing his ground, but his shoulders sagged, his lips quivered, and he wept.

"It's going to be okay," said Jenaro, leading him across the dirty carpet to rest on the sofa, until Wane cried himself out. Jenaro realized his friend felt remorse over his wife's death. "Wane, you were asleep. Lilly passed away quietly. Don't you think you would have awakened if she had called out?"

Shaking his head, he said, "No, no. I'm a deep... fuck," He swiped away tears from his face. "I'm a deep sleeper," he croaked with a lump in his throat. "Unless Lilly was screaming her head off, I wouldn't have heard her." Tears again filled his eyes.

Jenaro grabbed him by the shoulders. "Listen to me," he implored. "According to the medical examiner, it was a quick death. It's likely she never woke up. It was *not* your fault."

Wane let out deep, mournful sobs.

Jenaro's heart broke.

"Have a good cry, my friend. Let it all out."

When he calmed down, Jenaro said, "Come on, let's get this place in order." Together, the two old friends quietly cleaned up the mess.

After they dried and put away the dishes, vacuumed the floor, and stowed the garbage in the bin, Jenaro said, "Go upstairs and take a nice hot shower. It'll do you good. And while you're at it, shave that mug of yours. You look like a hobo."

Wane almost smiled and slowly climbed the stairs to the bathroom. An hour later, he emerged freshly bathed and shaved, dressed in clean clothes, and feeling lighter in both posture and spirit.

Jenaro prepared a can of chicken noodle soup, the only food, besides cookies and potato chips, in Wane's cupboard. He thought it best not to encourage Wane's bad eating habits by microwaving one of many prepared food packages in the freezer.

While Wane ate his soup, Jenaro began his month-long crusade to convince him to move. "Wane, why don't you give up this apartment and move to Coral Bells? It's nice in the Poconos."

When he got no reply, Jenaro pushed on. "This apartment has too many memories keeping you locked in a constant state of depression."

Wane slurped his soup, saying nothing.

Jenaro persisted. "When Carmen passed, I sensed her everywhere. I had to get away or lose my mind. I missed her so much."

Wane stopped eating and gave Jenaro a pained look. His lips quivered, and he whispered, "I do not want to leave my beloved Lilly behind."

"You will never leave her behind, Wane. She will always be with you, but you can't go on living this way."

After a few weeks, Jenaro's persuasive arguments finally convinced him, and Wane ended up at Coral Bells, where Jenaro kept an eye on him.

———

HARDLY ANY RESIDENTS at the Coral Bells Adult Living apartments suffer from poor health. Most are enjoying their golden years with minimal issues. They fill their days with community activities—socializing, exercising, taking dance or cooking lessons, or playing a round of golf at a nearby course. Monthly trips to area casinos, shopping sprees, or a bus ride into New York City for discounted Broadway shows are organized. During the Christmas holiday, many of the residents never miss catching the bus into the city to take in their favorite show at Radio City Music Hall. These seniors are enjoying their lives after decades of working hard, raising families, and putting themselves last.

At Coral Bells, Wane Rudolph reluctantly engaged in activities as much as his bulk would comfortably allow. "Exercise will help you with depression," Jenaro said, "and as a bonus, you'll get rid of that gut," he quipped.

Wane had occasionally tried exercising on Lilly's advice, but even walking a few blocks, winded him, so he gave up. At Coral Bells, he again tried walking for a few days so Wane would get off his back about physical activity. Having given that up, he tried a water aerobics class but left the pool halfway through the lesson. He liked to watch others swim and play tennis or bocce ball, activities his doctor had suggested would help him with weight loss and boost his overall physical condition, but Wane understood he wasn't the type to exert himself. He preferred to spend his time playing cards and board games or attending bible studies.

A little over five months at his new residence, Wane Rudolph suffered a cardiac event, leaving the hospital without permitting bypass surgery.

Believing immersing himself in the Holy Book would save him, he tried to take over the bible studies class he never failed to attend. With his extensive knowledge of religious history and penchant for arguing, he soon succeeded, ruffling more than a few feathers. With control over the class, he wrongly believed the group would want to meet more often. But try as he may, convincing the attendees to meet more than once a week proved futile. They had other interests to keep them busy.

After Wane's heart attack, Jenaro tried to convince Wane to at least try shuffleboard, a game requiring little exertion, but Wane wasn't interested.

"Well, if you're not even willing to try playing outdoor games, or even continue the water aerobics class, which, by the way, is a wonderful exercise for overall health, how about going to the cooking class with me?" Jenaro said hoping to get Wane out of the doldrums. "It won't help you get exercise, but at least you'll learn how to eat well. Besides, the instructor is terrific."

"No, thank you," Wane said.

"What else you got going on around here? Couch potatoing, perhaps?" Jenaro jested.

"Smart ass," Wane said, not appreciating the joke.

"Come on. One lesson won't kill you."

Wane didn't like to try new things lest he wound up hating them, but boredom and Jenaro's enthusiasm convinced him to try the class.

"Okay, I'll go see what's got you so worked up."

At the end of the first lesson, Wane discovered he loved to cook, sadly realizing for the first time how much effort his wife had put into preparing their meals.

A few weeks later, with eight lessons under his belt, he was planning a dinner party. It pleased Jenaro the cooking classes helped lift his friend out of his ennui. When Wane asked for his help with the preparations, he readily volunteered.

"Don't forget to choose the freshest ingredients at the market," Wane had instructed the evening before the party, barely containing his excitement. "I'd go myself, but I still have to choose the table linen, wine glasses, centerpiece, and fill out the seating cards—all those formal details people attend to when planning a meal for guests."

Jenaro hadn't seen his buddy this happy in a long time. *After what he's gone through*, he thought, *Wane deserves to be happy.* He set his alarm early to meet Wane at his apartment for breakfast and to pick up the grocery list.

By the time he began taking cooking lessons, Wane had become increasingly concerned with his health, feeling tired all the time, and nodding off in the middle of a conversation. The cooking class kept his mind from thinking about it. Because of fear, he stubbornly let time go by until he could no longer deny he needed help and contacted his doctor.

Because Wane had declined bypass surgery after his heart attack, his cardiologist suggested he stay overnight at the hospital hooked up to equipment monitoring his sleep pattern. "Your breathing does not sound good," he said after examining Wane. "Perhaps the results of your sleep test will convince you to have the surgery."

Wane agreed to the test so his doctor would stop pestering him about the bypass.

The morning after the most uncomfortable night Wane ever had, with electrodes attached to his head and body, he nervously listened to his diagnosis. The doctor did not mince words.

"Mr. Rudolph, your test results reveal you stop breathing at least twenty times every hour during sleep. This is a serious threat to your health."

Wane squirmed in his seat.

"You're suffering from Obstructive Sleep Apnea. That, combined with your coronary heart disease, puts you in grave danger of suffering another cardiac episode, which could lead to death. I suggest you try a CPAP machine to help you get a good night's sleep without interruption."

Wane could hardly believe he stopped breathing so many times during the night. His fear of dying in his sleep convinced him. "All right, doc. I'll try that …what's it called?"

"A Continuous Positive Airway Pressure machine, or CPAP."

"Okay."

"I also recommend you let me schedule the surgery. I promise you'll feel better after the operation."

Wane's eyes looked everywhere but at the doctor's face.

"Mr. Rudolph?"

"All right," he finally said. "I'll have the surgery."

Certain he had followed directions, Wane found it difficult to sleep wearing a mask connected to a tube, pumping air into his lungs. The first time he put on the full-face mask and turned on the machine, the rush of air felt like he was suffocating. In a panic, he ripped it off and switched the machine off. The doctor advised this might happen if he did not correctly set the right air pressure. Fidgeting with the settings confused him, but after a while, he got comfortable enough with the airflow to leave the mask on without ripping it off his face. The next night, determined to keep the mask on, he closed his eyes and instantly fell asleep. Fatigue from sleepless nights relaxed him into a deep slumber for the last time.

3

With no time to waste, he undid the buttons of his slicker and reached into the inside pocket to pull out a pair of latex gloves. Taking the stairs two at a time to the third floor, he tried fitting them on, but they stuck to his damp fingers. Cupping his hands over his mouth, he blew on them, warming his fingers enough to pull the gloves on. At the far end of the corridor, he stopped in front of Suite 323, Wane Rudolph's apartment.

Looking around to make sure he was alone, he retrieved a key from the smaller inside pocket of his coat. About to insert it into the lock, a very loud sneeze shook his entire body. He anxiously turned his head right and left, praying he had not given himself away. With the back of his hand, he swiped at his nose and took another quick look around. Hoping his victim was still fast asleep, he unlocked the door and silently closed it behind him. With his back against the door, he stuffed the key back into his pocket and cocked his head for any sound other than his heartbeat thumping in his ears. The air-conditioned apartment made him tremble, and he crossed his arms over his chest, trying to control his shaking.

A crack of lightning lit the kitchen a few feet from where he stood, momentarily paralyzing him. *I can't do this.*

Turning, he grabbed the doorknob, ready to abandon his plan, but another thought popped into his mind. *The bastard deserves it.* He let go of the doorknob, breathed deeply, and doggedly made his way down the dark corridor toward the bedroom.

Inching his way forward past the kitchen and living area, he carefully opened the bedroom door where Mr. Rudolph soundly slept to the steady rhythm of a CPAP machine, accompanied by the soothing sound of rain streaming down his windows.

There he is, sleeping, like an innocent man.

Standing at the foot of the bed, hate and anger sparked his courage. A nightlight guided him to the bathroom, where he grabbed a hand towel off the rack and flung it over his shoulder. He left the door ajar to make use of the nightlight. Wane Rudolph's rotund body lay on its left side, facing the CPAP machine on the nightstand. An old bible next to the machine caught his interest. He read the passage underlined in blue ink —*Forgive us for doing wrong, as we forgive others. Matthew 6:12.*

The trespasser sneered and turned his attention to the CPAP machine. In case Mr. Rudolph stirred, he kept his eye on him while he studied it. When he thought he had an idea how it worked, he turned the knob, simultaneously holding down the ramp and wheel buttons, adjusting the airflow to what he thought was its highest air pressure setting. The machine beeped a few times when it reached the maximum. He turned toward his victim ready to act, but the sleeping man did not appear to have heard anything. The prowler then planted his feet firmly on the floor and reached for him.

A stronger airflow rushing through the tubing pulled him out of deep sleep. Wane Rudolph somnolent, gasped and instinctively tugged at the mask covering his nose and mouth. When he was roughly flipped onto his back, his eyes sprung wide open, plunging him into what his confused mind thought was a nightmare.

A ghostly figure stood over him, and before he could work out what was happening, he felt intense pressure on his face and chest. The mask dug painfully into his face, and his chest felt as if it had a weight on it. Wane desperately clawed at the hand pushing down on his mask. He thrashed from side to side, his blood pressure skyrocketing to a dangerous level, but the person holding him down kept him in place. Confusion and his inability to fight off his attacker, and the air he was gulping, gave him the sensation of suffocating.

Terrified, with his last ounce of strength, he pushed down on the mattress with both hands and tried to lift himself off the bed. Never saying a word, his tormentor kept pressing down on his chest with one hand applying pressure to the mask with the other. With his energy depleted, Mr. Rudolph stopped struggling and prayed for a quick death. He was no match for the man holding him down. When he stopped fighting for his life, his executioner sensed the end was near, and whispered, "Goodbye, you son of a bitch."

A tear escaped Wane's eye. *Why...* but before he could finish the thought, his heart gave out.

A feeling of urgency struck the murderer. *Gotta get out of here.*

He set the machine back to its original numbers and sat next to the body, not troubled by the dead man's unseeing eyes. He removed the mask, and with the hand towel, swiftly dabbed the sweat and spittle from his victim's neck, and bald head. He slung the towel back over his shoulder when he finished. After readjusting the mask on his face, he turned the body back onto its left side and pulled the bedcovers over the corpse.

The killer tore off the gloves and tossed them into the waste-basket in the bathroom. He then flung the towel in the direction of the laundry hamper. Gently pulling the front door open, he sneaked a peek into the empty hallway and stepped out, forgetting to reach into his pocket for the key.

———

JENARO MILLER KNOCKED on Mr. Rudolph's door. Not getting an answer, he knocked louder, thinking his friend might still be asleep. After a few tries, he became concerned and instinctively reached for the doorknob.

Huh? Wane left the door unlocked?

Jenaro didn't think Wane expected anyone else that morning, but perhaps he had enlisted another resident to help with the preparations for the dinner party.

When he stepped into the dark apartment, Jenaro immediately discarded the notion Wane had a visitor. He flicked on the ceiling light and noticed wet smudges on the floor, which added to his apprehension. "Wane, it's me, Jenaro. Are you all right?" he called out.

Getting no reply, he rushed toward the bedroom and breathed a sigh of relief. His friend rested in bed, wearing his CPAP mask.

Jenaro smiled. *Better let him sleep a while longer.*

He thought he'd clean the floor and headed toward the kitchen to find a mop, but the nightlight drew his attention. A hand towel on the floor next to the hamper gave him a queasy feeling warning him something was wrong. He flung the towel into the hamper and hurried over to the bed to check on Mr. Rudolph. The unexpected, unlocked door and the wet floor had disturbed Jenaro, but that towel sent his nervous system into a frenzy.

He gently shook Mr. Rudolph's shoulder. "Wane?"

Getting no reaction, Jenaro shook him a bit more forcefully, inadvertently moving him onto his back.

"Oh my God!" he blurted when he saw his unseeing eyes.

Jenaro tore out of the apartment and down the stairs, almost tripping over his own feet. "Help!" he yelled, running through the lobby. All conversation ceased, and everyone simultaneously turned their heads at the panicked man.

"Something's happened to Mr. Rudolph. Please, someone, call an ambulance."

The handyman stuck his head out of the coffee room and dialed 911 on his cell phone. "I'm on it," he yelled.

When the paramedics arrived, Jenaro directed them to Apartment 323. He helplessly stood outside the bedroom door, fighting back tears as EMTs examined the body, immediately recognizing the patient had expired. Jenaro bawled when one of them pulled out his cell phone and called the police.

Waiting for news, residents gathered in the lobby. When the police and the coroner arrived, a collective gasp spread throughout the crowd.

The coroner examined the body and recorded the time of death. He determined Mr. Rudolph died from natural causes, probably because of a myocardial infarction.

Fond memories of the dearly-departed circulated when they removed the body, even from those who did not care for him, the killer commiserating along with them.

Jenaro and his old friend, Wane, had designated one another as trustees to their will. It now fell to him to fulfill his duties.

———

THAT EVENING, the killer wrapped in a blanket despite the warm and muggy night, fitfully dozed. After a particularly long coughing fit, he got out of bed, pajamas sticking to his feverish skin. In the kitchen, he opened the cupboard and coaxed a couple of aspirins out of the bottle and into his palm. He opened the fridge and reached for a beer, his fourth since coming home after an exhausting day. The screw-on cap dropped to the floor when he twisted it, but he scarcely noticed. All he wanted was to take a long swig to cool his parched throat. Washing down the aspirins with an entire bottle of beer, he went into the living room and plopped down on his recliner, grabbing the throw blanket on the couch to cover himself.

Soon his mind conjured the image of those terror-filled eyes. He thought killing the man responsible for his unhappiness would rid him of all those emotions he'd carried with him for so many years—feelings of anger, hatred, loss, and heartbreak, but those feelings remained a part of him. *Perhaps I'll never be happy,* he thought and drifted off to sleep.

———

WHEN he first heard Wane Rudolph's voice joking with his fellow card players in the game room, he did a double take. Rudolph had gotten a lot older than the last time he saw him, but his voice was the same. He wanted to grab Rudolph by the throat and choke the life out of him right then and there. It took all he had to control the rage clouding his judgment, almost running out of the game room before he gave into his baser instincts.

Since that day, whenever he was around Wane Rudolph, his hands became sweaty, his heart beat faster, and anxiety coursed through his body. After a few weeks, he knew what he had to do.

Dawn found him passed out in his lounger.

4

*H*oward Pierce eased up on the accelerator a few yards behind the blue Rav4, traveling south on Route 209 in Marshalls Creek. The vehicle took the ramp onto Route 80 East. Crossing the Delaware Water Gap Bridge into New Jersey, he groaned. Pierce hated driving on Route 80, where drivers did eighty on eighty as the popular catchphrase went. Fortunately, traffic remained light this early afternoon hour, causing him to hang back further while keeping the Toyota in view.

The private investigator believed his target hadn't noticed the tail. He hoped the baseball cap and sunglasses he sported would dissuade any suspicion if, by chance, the man he followed paid attention to the sparse traffic behind him. If made, Pierce would have to give up the pursuit for today. He normally didn't get close to his mark, but on the insistence of the woman who hired him, he'd taken a chance that morning, sipping his coffee at the same cafe the wayward husband frequented in case he met up with a paramour.

Pierce hated cheating-spouse-surveillance cases. These investigations made him feel uncomfortable, like a voyeur. But if he turned down these kinds of cases, he would exclude a lucrative part of his business.

Over the past four days, he'd spent countless hours waiting to catch the subject in a compromising situation. So far, he had nothing suspicious to report. The daily schedule the missus had provided for her husband appeared perfectly normal. He worked two jobs locally, one as a car salesman, and the other teaching computer skills two evenings a week at the high school. He appeared not to spend time with any friends, be they male or female. After work, if he wasn't out and about running errands, he went straight home, where he stayed all evening.

The Toyota's right-turn signal blinked a few yards before the exit ramp. The private investigator breathed a sigh of relief. He wasn't heading deeper into New Jersey, or heaven forbid, all the way to New York City.

Pierce followed as the Rav4 exited the highway and onto Route 46. He almost lost sight of it when an RV leaving a gas station forced its way onto the road in front of him. He slowed down to give himself enough wiggle room to exit if the Toyota turned early.

The blinker flashed again as the Rav4 approached the exit and drove for a few minutes before entering the Super 8 Motel's parking lot.

Pierce parked and grabbed the camera case from the passenger seat. Retrieving the Nikon, he got out of the car as the subject climbed the motel's exterior stairs near the parking lot. On the second level, the man nervously looked around before knocking on the door of room 208 in the middle of the hallway. Pierce stepped back far enough for a better view. Camera-ready, he pointed it and peered through the telephoto lens, expertly adjusting the aperture. With his finger already positioned over the shutter button, he pressed down as soon as a young woman dressed in a tight-fitting, provocative dress opened the door.

click, click, click, click

He released the shutter when the door closed behind them.

Pierce got into his car and drove it to a space where he would have a better view. He had witnessed these rendezvous too many times during his brief career as a private investigator. They usually lasted about an hour. After jotting down the time of the encounter on his pad, he reached for his lunch bag and unwrapped a ham and cheese sandwich his wife had prepared for him. He poured himself a cup of coffee from his thermos, turned on the car radio, and ate his lunch, humming along to the oldies. When he finished eating, he stepped out of the car and stretched his legs, all the while he watched that room.

Forty-five minutes later, the door to room 208 opened. Ready, Pierce once again held down the shutter. Through the lens, he witnessed a deep-throated kiss and a tight embrace—the money shot.

These photographs, no matter how much she wanted the truth, would hurt the suspicious wife. But she hired him to uncover infidelity, and she deserved a full report. It was not up to him to judge, no matter how distasteful the job.

———

IN 2007, Howard Pierce was feeling bored. Two and a half years after he retired from the Force, he'd fixed everything that needed fixing in and around his home, helped with the gardening, and learned how to cook a few dishes. There was nothing left for him to do. While he enjoyed traveling with his wife, Louise, they couldn't keep touring forever, nor was Pierce the hobbyist type, as Louise suggested he take up to fill his time. Truth is, he missed police work.

Sitting in his den one morning ready to play another computer card game, an ad popped up for a private detective agency in Philadelphia. *Private Investigator?* he thought.

Pierce abandoned his plans for Solitaire and explored the private eye field for the rest of the afternoon.

Weeks later, with his brand new license in hand, he visited a real estate office and found the perfect space—two rooms, one hundred square foot office, on the second floor of a two-story building off of Courthouse Square. After signing the lease, he wasted no time shopping for office furniture.

Pierce opened Bloodhound Investigations, feeling the happiest he'd been since his retirement. On that first day of business, he stood in front of his brand new door admiring the fancy etched lettering and ran a finger along the company's name.

Although cops would never admit it, superstitions and belief in good luck charms had always been part of police rituals. Touching the agency's name became Pierce's practice before entering his office.

He smirked at the irony of his choice in selecting the business name, a title given to him by a psychotic killer during his last homicide investigation as the lead detective at the Stroud Area Regional Police Department. That woman had enjoyed taunting Pierce, using the name *bloodhound* to refer to him in her pithy notes and jarring messages.

Pierce took pride in ownership of the nickname that had once been used to ridicule him. *Thank you, Miss Gil. May you forever enjoy your new abode, courtesy of the Commonwealth.*

He entered the anteroom where clients were first seen and scheduled by his assistant, Ruby. Her desk faced the door, a wooden chair positioned next to it. One of four colorful lithographs hung on the wall behind Ruby's desk. Pierce's wife had insisted on adorning the office with cheerful images. She claimed it calmed agitated clients that might have trouble expressing themselves. A wall clock Ruby bought as an office warming present hung in between the lithographs.

On the left side near the entrance, Louise had placed a coat tree, fearing her husband would have nailed pegs on the beautiful brick wall.

The Mr. Coffee machine sat on a table in the far corner near the room's only window. A small refrigerator placed alongside the coffee machine was Ruby's idea, so they could both bring lunch from home. She filled it with yogurt cups, fruit, cream for the coffee, and a few bottles of water, leaving just enough space for their lunch. Two file cabinets took up the room's remaining free space.

Ruby greeted Pierce when he entered. As was her custom, she had arrived fifteen minutes before him and was already at her desk going over the day's agenda. "Good morning, boss."

Pierce was used to Ruby's frequent and dramatic changes to her hair. At least he thought so. But her latest dye combination, a vivid red with stark blue highlights styled in thick, long curls, momentarily shocked him.

"Good morning, Ruby, love your hair," he said, not sure he liked her new look.

Smiling, she gently played with one of her curls. "Thank you. I love it too."

"Well, it suits you. Any messages?"

Ruby stopped twisting her hair and grabbed the pink message pad from her desk. "Yes. Detective Ramirez phoned a few minutes ago."

"Ramirez?" A smile spread across his face. Detective Ignacio (Iggy) Ramirez had been Pierce's second in command during his tenure on the detective squad. Not only a former colleague but a close friend and *compadre*. Pierce and his wife were godparents to Ramirez's son, Joaquin.

"Yes," said Ruby. "He left a number and asked if you would call him as soon as you came in. Sounded aggravated if you ask me." She ripped the page from the pad.

Aggravated? Pierce reached for the note Ruby held out to him. "Thanks. What's on the calendar for today?"

Ruby flipped open the appointment book on her desk. "Full day, boss. The first thing is the telephone meeting with the insurance company at nine-thirty. Then, Mrs. Paredes is coming in at eleven with her husband's salary information."

She ran her finger down the page. "Followed by Mr. and Mrs. Olivieri at twelve-thirty regarding the missing teen. After lunch, you have a meeting with Mr. Figueroa at two."

"Who?"

She looked up. "Mr. Figueroa is an insurance claims adjuster. He wants you to look into possible insurance fraud. I squeezed him in for this afternoon."

Pierce nodded. "Okay."

"You asked me to remind you to pick up the bench warrants at the magistrate's office. You can do that after you meet with Mr. Figueroa."

"Yes. thanks. I need to get there before they close, and serve them in the morning, first thing," said Pierce.

"Also, remember to give me the information for the attorney representing the father in the Sullivan child custody dispute so I can type it up all nice and pretty." She giggled.

Pierce laughed.

"The attorney needs your findings by tomorrow," she added and closed the book.

"All right. I'll call Ramirez, then I'll get to everything else." He reached into his briefcase. "Here are my notes on today's surveillance case."

Ruby took his pad. "I'll type a draft for you to finalize."

"Thanks. There's no hurry. I'm not meeting Mrs. Lebron until tomorrow."

"You know me, boss. I don't like putting things off."

"Yeah, I know." he smiled and sniffed the air. "Mm, freshly brewed. Think I'll grab a cup before making that call."

"Careful you don't go over your limit, or I'll have to report your infraction to Mrs. Pierce," Ruby teased.

Pierce placed his hand over his heart and promised. "Last cup this morning."

"Heard that before," replied Ruby, turning toward her computer.

Pierce laughed and reached for the coffeepot. With a twinge of self-reproach, he filled his mug halfway. He'd already had his usual two cups at breakfast.

In his office, Pierce blew on the surface of the coffee before taking a sip. "That's what I'm talking about," he muttered, placing the mug reluctantly on his desk. He then rolled his chair out from beneath the desk, slumped down on it, and reached for the phone.

Ramirez picked up on the first ring.

"Hey, Iggy. It's Howard. What's up?"

"Thanks for calling back, Howard."

"Sure thing. Is something wrong? My assistant thought you sounded aggravated when you called earlier."

"Sorry about that. It's been a Murphy's Law kinda week. Please apologize if she thought I was rude. You know how it is."

"Indeed, I do," Pierce said, chuckling. "I'm sure she didn't think you were rude, but I'll give her your apology."

"I appreciate that."

"So, what's up?"

"I want to run something by you, Sarge."

Iggy, addressing him by his former rank, pleased him. He put the phone on speaker and relaxed in his chair. "I'm listening."

"There was a death at the Coral Bells Adult Living apartments yesterday morning."

"Yes, Louise mentioned it."

"Coroner said the deceased suffered a heart attack."

"But foul play may have been involved?" asked Pierce.

"Well, you tell me. Last evening, a call came in from a Mr. Jenaro Miller, a resident at the apartments. He said he discovered the body when he let himself into the decedent's unlocked apartment to pick up a grocery list."

"Did Mr. Rudolph normally leave his door unlocked?" asked Pierce.

"Miller admitted his friend had once forgotten to engage the lock, but remembered before going to bed. Although concerned, he didn't think this had become a habit. He had been running errands for Mr. Rudolph ever since his first heart attack, and Rudolph had always unlocked his door to let him in. They were good friends who knew each other before moving to Coral Bells. Anyway, when Miller turned on the light and stepped into the apartment he noticed the floor wet and smudged. When he checked on Rudolph, he thought he was asleep and did not disturb him. Miller intended to mop the mess in the foyer when he spotted a towel on the bathroom floor."

"Is the towel of any consequence?"

"From how Miller described his friend, he was a neat freak who would never have left a towel on the floor. Miller panicked, certain something bad had happened. When he tried to wake Rudolph, he realized he was dead. He high-tailed it to the lobby screaming something had happened to his friend, forgetting about the unlocked door, wet floor, and the towel."

"Hmm."

"Miller said his friend's death shook him up pretty bad, and it wasn't until last evening he remembered the condition of Rudolph's apartment when he discovered the body. That's when he called us."

Howard's analytical mind kicked in listening to the sergeant. Solving this kind of enigma had been his life's work, a skill he'd been good at, and he hoped he would be involved in a more investigative role other than surveilling a suspect or doing background checks for the department.

"By the time first responders, police, and the coroner vacated the premises, all of them had smudged the floor with their wet shoes, Howard, so *that* piece of information is useless."

"Yeah."

"Miller was too upset to listen to reason, hence my phone call to you, pal."

"Okay. Anything else?"

"That's it in a nutshell."

Pierce combed his hair with his fingers and casually said, "Not much there, Iggy. I take it you'd like me to talk to Miller?"

"Would you mind? He was adamant something sinister was at play. If anyone can prove an unlocked door, wet floor, and a carelessly dropped towel are clues of a homicide, it's you, buddy."

Pierce laughed. "No need for ass-kissing, Iggy. I'm happy to help."

"Hey, I'm sincere," he chortled.

"In that case, thanks for the compliment."

"No, thank *you*, Sarge. We're up to our necks in paperwork and can't spare the time to investigate a seemingly natural death. I'll email Miller's contact info to you soon as I hang up."

"Okay," Pierce said, smiling when Iggy again called him Sarge.

"How's Linda and Joaquin?" he asked.

"Good. Louise and the girls?"

"All fine. Why don't we get together soon? It's been a while."

"Yes. I'll let Linda set it up with Louise."

"All right."

"Goodbye, pal, and thanks again."

"Any time, Iggy."

Keenly paying attention to everything Sergeant Ramirez had described, Pierce understood he had his work cut out for him if he were to prove a homicide.

He picked up the coffee cup and took a sip of the lukewarm

coffee, but he didn't mind. He hadn't felt this excited since opening up his business.

After printing Ramirez's email, He dialed Mr. Miller.

"Hello."

"Mr. Miller?"

"This is he. Who's calling?"

"I'm a private investigator working with the police. Sergeant Ramirez asked me to call. He said you have information regarding Mr. Wane Rudolph's death."

"Yes. Thank you for calling."

"I'd like to meet with you to go over your concerns, if I may."

"Yes. I live at the Coral Bells Adult Living apartments. Know the place?"

For the past few years, Pierce's wife volunteered at Coral Bells, teaching cooking lessons twice a week. Pierce had never been there but knew the location.

"Yes, sir. What's the apartment number?"

"Apartment 408."

Pierce jotted down the number and asked, "Is this afternoon convenient, say around 2:30?"

"Yes, thank you. What name should I leave with the desk?"

Pierce used his first name when undercover in case he ran into someone familiar, who might call him Howard, in front of a subject. In such a case, he would not have to think twice before responding. Once he meets with Mr. Miller, he'll reveal his true identity.

"Howard Martal," Pierce said, a name he had used more than once.

"Goodbye, Mr. Martal, and thank you again."

"You're welcome. See you this afternoon."

Pierce poked his head out his office door. "Ruby, please cancel my two o'clock with that insurance adjuster. I've just set up another meeting at two-thirty with Mr. Jenaro Miller at the Coral Bells Adult Living apartments."

"All right. I'll reschedule Mr. Figueroa and put Mr. Miller in the book."

"Thanks. Did you finish typing my notes for the insurance company?"

Ruby reached for a manila folder on her desk, momentarily mesmerizing him when her curls swayed with the movement of her head. "All in there."

He walked over to her desk. Grabbing the folder, he said, "You're a peach, Ruby."

She beamed. "I know I am," and picked up the phone to reschedule Figueroa's appointment.

Pierce leafed through the folder and checked the wall clock. *I have time to review this before my call.*

He headed back into his office to prepare for the insurance company and forced himself to concentrate on his notes when all he wanted to do was investigate a homicide.

5

*H*aving canceled his two o'clock meeting, Pierce had time after lunch to pick up the bench warrants before heading over to Coral Bells.

He arrived thirty minutes early for his meeting with Mr. Miller, giving him time to check out the outdoor amenities before entering the apartment building. Louise had told him how much she admired the well-groomed grounds. Looking around at the plantings and manicured lawns, he had to agree.

With his detective's eye for detail, he canvassed the area from the left side of the parking lot as he faced the building, circling until he arrived at the entrance.

More than once, he passed a small group of people power-walking. At the tennis courts, he watched a doubles match, impressed at the game's fast pace. Men in white shorts, and women wearing brightly colored tennis skirts ran around the court as if decades younger, despite the scorching August sun. Pierce watched for a few minutes, his forehead beaded with perspiration running down his temples. He reached in his pocket for the clean handkerchief he always carried since his rookie days when a teen he chased threw dirt in his face. With nothing to wipe off the dirt, he had to wait until he put the teen in handcuffs and got back to the precinct to wash his irritated eyes. On his day off, he bought a dozen handkerchiefs and never left home without a couple in his pocket.

At the swimming pool, a water aerobics class was in session. The class, made up of mostly women bobbing in the water in their bathing caps, obediently followed the instructions of a tall and tanned, daunting-looking man in a bathing suit and flowered shirt. He stood on the deck holding a microphone and barking orders. "Mabel, raise those arms higher. Atta girl," he called out when she complied.

Pierce turned his attention away from the instructor to the people relaxing on deck chairs, reading, sunning, or watching the activity in the pool, eager for the class to end for their turn to swim in the cool water. One couple, who looked to be in their eighties, lay side-by-side on their lounge chairs, engaged in conversation, holding hands, and gazing into each other's eyes. Pierce smiled, thinking of Louise.

At the bocce ball and shuffleboard courts, he again admired the stamina of the people in their headbands and shorts, not caring about thinning hair, sagging skin, or varicose veins. Checking his watch, he saw he still had ten minutes before he met with Mr. Miller. He pulled himself away after someone rolled his bocce ball to within a hair's breadth from the pallino ball. Everyone cheered, including a couple who abandoned their shuffleboard game and ran over when they heard the commotion.

About to push the button on the intercom, a woman pulled open the door to the right of him and entered the building. Pierce followed. The air-conditioned air felt wonderful against his hot, sweaty skin. All business, Pierce headed toward the receptionist's desk.

"May I help you?" she asked with a friendly smile.

"Yes, I'm here to visit Mr. Miller in apartment 408. My name is Howard Martal."

"One moment, please," she said with a friendly smile.

Looking through her log book, she found the entry and turned the book toward Pierce. "Sign here please."

Pierce scrawled the name Martel and checked his watch for the time before filling it in.

The receptionist swiveled her chair around, pointed, and said, "Take the elevator on the right to the fourth floor."

"Thank you," Pierce said, but before heading toward the elevator, he asked, "Are the front doors usually unlocked?"

"Only during the day. Our residents are in and out all day long. They get annoyed if they have to ring the doorbell or use their key," she chuckled.

Pierce smiled. "When are the doors locked?"

"They lock the doors at ten until seven the next morning. After lockdown, residents use their key or get buzzed in, but they're usually tucked in for the night by then."

Reading Monica Jefferson on her name tag, Pierce asked, "Who locks the doors, Miss Jefferson?"

Biting her bottom lip, Monica looked as if she shouldn't have given a stranger so much information should he be casing the place.

Reading her worried expression, Pierce said, "Mr. Miller and I are old friends. He's told me many times how nice this place is. After my visit, perhaps I'll look around."

"Really?" she asked with interest, all thoughts of a robbery vanishing.

"Yes. Jenaro talked me into checking out this place when I mentioned I'd like to move closer to my job at ESU. He's sure I'm going to love it here."

"I agree. This is a wonderful place. I don't live here myself. Can't afford it, but everyone seems happy."

"Jenaro certainly is," Pierce said.

"Are you a teacher?" she asked.

"Yes. I teach an astronomy course," he said, not knowing if such a course was taught at the university.

"Science was never one of my best subjects. I preferred history."

Pierce nodded.

Perhaps because Mr. Rudolph's death was fresh on her mind, Monica lowered her voice and asked, "Did Mr. Miller tell you of Mr. Rudolph's death?"

"Yes. Jenaro's taking it badly. They were close friends."

A man walked through reception on his way out. Monica put up her index finger in a gesture to Pierce to wait a moment. She called out to him. "Good afternoon, Mr. Anderson. Enjoy your walk."

The man answered with a scowl that made Monica smile. She turned to Pierce. "I love telling him to enjoy his walk because he always makes a funny face. Makes my day."

Pierce smiled.

"What were we talking about? Oh yes, Mr. Rudolph. Poor man. They say he had a heart attack," She leaned forward and whispered, "but Mr. Miller doesn't believe it."

Pierce worried Miller had told everyone of his skepticism, perhaps alerting someone who may have been responsible for his friend's death. "Did he tell you that?" he asked.

Monica again bit her lip, no doubt worried he may think her a gossiper.

Pierce saved her from an explanation. "Not to worry, Miss Jefferson."

"Please, call me Monica. Everyone around here does."

"Monica, when someone passes away suddenly, sometimes friends or family members find it difficult to face the loss, and look for reasons other than natural causes."

"Yeah, that makes sense," she said.

"So, who locks up for the night?"

"The security guard on duty."

Pierce glanced at his watch—2:27 p.m. "When is your shift over?"

"I'm here until four. Why?"

"Can we talk after I meet with my friend?"

"I guess so," she said.

Pierce heard the uncertainty in her voice. "Thanks. I'd like to know how they run this place from someone other than a salesperson."

Monica smiled. "I'd be happy to answer your questions."

"Thanks, Monica. See you later."

Pierce, alias Martal, turned toward the elevator.

———

WHEN THEY WERE SEATED, Pierce said, "Mr. Miller, as I mentioned on the telephone, I'm a private investigator working with the police. My real name is Howard Pierce. I run Bloodhound Investigations. If I'm to look into Mr. Rudolph's death, I'd prefer it if no one here knows who I am."

"Of course. I understand," said Jenaro Miller.

"Would you like a cup of coffee, Mr. Pierce? I mean, Mr. Martal," asked Jenaro with a quiver in his voice.

Pierce recognized the grief in Miller's voice and bloodshot eyes. "Call me Howard. Easier to remember."

"Thank you. Would you like a cup of coffee, Howard?"

"Thank you, no. I've already exceeded my coffee allotment for today," he grinned. "My wife, Louise, got me down to four cups a day from my ten or more cups when I was on the Force."

"Louise Pierce? Is she the same Mrs. Pierce, who gives cooking lessons here?"

"She is."

"Mrs. Pierce is a talented cook and an excellent teacher."

"Thank you. My wife loves to cook, and I love to eat," Pierce said with a wide grin.

Miller smiled weakly. "Wane's wife was also a wonderful cook, but in all the years I knew him, he never showed an interest in cooking until I encouraged him to take Mrs. Pierce's cooking class. Wane wanted to show off what he learned, and planned a dinner party for last ..." His smile faded.

Pierce thought it best to begin the interview. Miller looked as if he would cry at any moment.

"All right," Pierce said, flipping open his pad. "Tell me what happened yesterday morning."

Miller breathed deeply. "Like I told the police, Wane was having a dinner party last evening. He asked me to do the grocery shopping for him, so I came by early to pick up the list."

"What time was that?"

"I knocked on Wane's door at 7:30."

"Is that the time you both agreed you'd come by?" Pierce asked, jotting down the time.

"Yes. Wane suggested we have breakfast together to go over any last-minute details, and to make sure the shopping list was complete."

"Did you have a key to Mr. Rudolph's apartment?"

"Not then, no. I knocked and when he didn't come to the door, I called out to him. I thought he'd be up and ready when I arrived. When he didn't answer, I instinctively turned the door-knob, surprised when the door opened."

"Did Mr. Rudolph usually forget to lock his door?"

"Not that he mentioned. Oh, except for that one time, but he remembered before retiring for the night."

"Perhaps he had his plans for the dinner party on his mind and he simply forgot to lock up," Pierce said.

"I don't think he forgot. I think someone broke in," Miller said.

"What makes you think so?"

"Little things."

"Such as?"

"When I walked into his apartment, I flipped the light switch and noticed wet smudges on the floor as if someone had walked on it after being out in that rain storm we were having." He lowered his head and began rubbing his hands together.

Pierced imagined he did not want to relive finding his friend dead in his bed. He waited a few seconds and asked, "What did you do next?"

Miller looked up. "The dirty floor puzzled me, and I called out for Wane."

"Why were you puzzled?" Pierce asked. "It had been raining all night and into the morning. Perhaps Mr. Rudolph went out and when he came back dripped water on the floor from his wet raincoat or umbrella."

Miller shook his head emphatically. "Even if Wane had been out in the rain, he never would have gone to bed without wiping the floor. When it concerned his housework, Wane was fastidious. He would never leave the floor in that condition."

"All right. Then what did you do?"

"When he didn't answer, I went into his bedroom to check on him. He looked to be asleep, so I did not disturb him. I meant to go to the kitchen to grab a mop, but the nightlight in the bathroom caught my eye. I walked into the bathroom and saw a towel lying on the floor. That's when I knew something was wrong."

"Why's that?" Pierce said, making a few notations on his pad.

Wane's jaw tightened, having to explain again what an orderly person Wane had been. He said, "Because Wane would've picked up the towel."

Pierce picked up on Miller's annoyance but suggested, "Perhaps he wasn't feeling well and after using the bathroom, absently dropped the towel."

"No, no," Jenaro said, raising his voice. "If he were not feeling well, he still would've cleaned up before going to bed. He was *that* meticulous. Taking the trouble to put on that mask before laying down tells me he wasn't ill."

"What mask?" Pierce asked.

"A CPAP mask for his sleep apnea. He'd only been using it for a couple of nights. If his doctor hadn't pressured him into it after his sleep test results, Wane would have fought against it. But, once he had it, he was determined to get accustomed to the darn mask, as he called it, even though he hated it. Bottom line, he agreed to that contraption because of his fear he would die in his sleep if he didn't listen to his doctor's advice."

Jenaro realized the irony of what he'd just said and breathed deeply to keep himself from crying.

"Take your time, Mr. Miller. I know this is difficult."

Jenaro swallowed hard.

When Miller regained his composure, Pierce said, "Tell me what you did when you saw the towel on the floor."

"I immediately went to shake Wane awake, gently at first, but when he didn't stir, I shook him a little harder." A single tear ran down his pale face. He quickly swiped it away with the back of a liver-spotted hand. "I realized he was dead when I looked into his eyes, but I ran to the lobby calling for help, hoping they could still save him," he said, lips trembling.

"Would you like a drink of water, Mr. Miller?"

"Yes. I just need a moment. Excuse me." After getting up, he pulled a paper towel out of the holder in the kitchen to blow his nose. He threw the towel into the trashcan and took a glass out of the cupboard to pour himself a drink from the faucet. He slowly drank, facing the sink.

Pierce watched Miller over the half wall that separated the kitchen and living rooms absentmindedly rubbing his chin. His gut told him there was something here to investigate, but he wasn't yet ready to take on the case with so little to go on.

Miller seemed calmer after his break. "Sorry about that," he said, taking his seat.

"No need for you to apologize."

"Do you think you can find out what really happened to my friend?" Miller asked timidly.

"I gotta tell you, Mr. Miller, there's not much here to suggest foul play. Is there anything else you remember?"

Miller creased his eyebrows and wrung his hands, trying to recall. "Oh, yes, now that you mention it. Yesterday, I asked Management to let me into Wane's apartment. They didn't allow me to stay there after they took him away." He sighed. "I wanted to clean up the mess in his bedroom and sort out his things."

"Mr. Rudolph had no relatives to take care of that for him?" Pierce asked.

"His wife died about a year and a half ago. He has a sister, but she lives in Scotland. Other than her, I don't know of any other relatives."

"Any children?"

"He had a son, Ethan, but he died at an early age."

Pierce jotted the name on his pad. "How did he die?"

Jenaro's gaze shifted away, not wanting to answer.

"Mr. Miller?"

He moaned … "Wane's son committed suicide when he was a teen."

Pierce shook his head. "How old was the boy?"

"Wane never said, only that he attended junior high school in the Bronx where they lived. I didn't know Wane then."

"Any idea where in the Bronx they lived?"

"Oh yes. They lived on 161st Street. That's where I met the Rudolphs when Carmen, my wife, and I moved into the building."

"What year was that?"

Miller puffed out his cheeks, blowing out a breath. "Let's

see. I moved to the Bronx from downtown Manhattan in the late eighties."

Pierce wrote on his pad. "Did Mr. Rudolph tell you what led to his son's suicide?"

"No. If he knew the reason, he didn't share it with me. It wasn't until we had known each other for a few years that Wane spoke of the tragedy one evening after he'd had a couple of drinks, but he never spoke of it again."

"I see. Did they let you in to take care of Mr. Rudolph's belongings?"

"Yes. Management approved it after I showed them the document Wane signed, making me executor of his will. They called Mace to let me into the apartment."

"Mace?"

"Yes, Mace, like the spice. He's our handyman."

Pierce scribbled the name. "Did Mace stay with you while you saw to Mr. Rudolph's possessions?"

"No. He let me in and left."

"Are the boxes still in Mr. Rudolph's apartment?"

"Yes. I have to call the Salvation Army to pick up most of them. Don't know what I'm going to do with his old photos and memorabilia."

"While seeing to Mr. Rudolph's belongings, did you find anything else that made you think he did not die a natural death?"

"That's what I was getting to. When I went to empty the trash in Wane's bathroom, a pair of latex gloves laid at the bottom of the basket."

"Is this unusual?"

"Yes. Wane was allergic to latex. No way he would have latex gloves in his home."

Pierce felt that familiar tickle in his stomach. *Finally, a viable piece of the puzzle.*

"Still have the gloves?"

"No. I put them in the trash this morning for pickup." He gasped. "Oh, my. I should've kept them as proof that someone left them in Wane's apartment."

Woulda been nice to lift fingerprints off those gloves, Pierce thought, but he said, "Don't worry about it, Mr. Miller."

"But the gloves would have proven I'm not lying."

"I believe you."

Miller relaxed. "Thank you."

"You're welcome. Now then. Did you find Mr. Rudolph's apartment key when you went back to gather his things?"

"Yes."

"Where did you find it?"

"It was in the dish on the kitchen counter where he usually put his keys and pocket change."

"On the morning of his death, did you see if the key was missing from the dish?"

"Oh, no. I never thought to look."

"That's understandable. If the key was in its usual place, perhaps Mr. Miller simply forgot to lock his door."

"Possibly, or someone could have jimmied the lock, or gotten hold of Wane's key somehow, and then replaced it after ..." He trailed off, looking away.

"Anything is possible, Mr. Miller."

"Mr. Pierce," he said. "I'm certain someone was in Wane's apartment the day he died. *I just know it.*"

Because he always listened to his gut, and because he longed to dive headfirst into a homicide investigation, Pierce said, "All right, Mr. Miller. I'll look into it."

Miller smiled faintly. "Thank you."

"You're welcome."

"One more thing. Please don't share your concerns with anyone in the building. If your suspicions turn out to be correct, and the killer lives or works here, you might alert him of your suspicions."

"Oh, dear, I told Monica, our receptionist, and a good friend of mine, Mrs. Garcia, that I didn't believe Wane died of a heart attack. I'm sorry. I didn't think."

Pierce felt bad he scared him, but it wouldn't do for Miller to go around alerting the person responsible for Rudolph's death. "Don't worry about it. The killer is probably long gone by now."

Miller blinked nervously. "I hope so."

Pierce thought he was probably worried about being killed in his bed, too. He changed the conversation.

"Have you made funeral arrangements for Mr. Rudolph?"

"What?"

"Have you made the funeral arrangements?"

"Wane stipulated in his will he wanted a church service and then straight to the crematorium. His service will take place next Monday at 9 a.m."

"If Mr. Miller didn't want a wake, why is the service scheduled a week after his death?"

"Wane's sister insists on flying in from Scotland even though she's in her eighties and in poor health. With the long travel time and layover, she will need a couple of days to recover. I thought it best to delay the service."

"I see. So Mr. Miller's body is still at the morgue?"

"Yes."

Pierce closed his pad. "You said you didn't have the key to Mr. Rudolph's apartment at the time you found his door open, but you have it now?"

"Yes. The manager let me keep it. There's still a lot to do before I return it."

"I'd like to look at Mr. Miller's apartment, if I may?"

"Yes, of course," Miller said, standing. "Let me get the key."

Rudolph's apartment opened into a hallway. Four feet to the left of the entrance, Miller pointed to the kitchen, where stacked cartons of Mr. Rudolph's things waited to be disposed of.

"As you see, I've already cleaned out the cabinets and drawers."

Pierce nodded.

"I intended to strip the bed and launder the sheets, but I couldn't bring myself to do so. Tomorrow, I'll take care of the bedroom."

Pierce thought perhaps finding the latex gloves filled him with dread.

Walking into the living room, Miller pointed, "The bedroom is through that door. If you don't mind, I'll wait for you here."

"No, of course not. I won't be long," said Pierce.

In the bedroom, Pierce lifted the bedcovers and inspected the pillows, noticing sweat stains. He kneeled and looked under the bed. When he straightened up, he examined the CPAP machine on the nightstand and inspected the attached hose and mask, taking notice of the machine's settings.

Putting the hose and mask in the position he'd found them, Pierce picked up the bible and read the underlined paragraph.

Forgiveness. What for?

He put the bible down and took out his pad and pen, copying the passage and jotting down the settings on the machine.

Mr. Rudolph's dresser and his closet were orderly, everything nicely put away. Pierce found nothing suspicious in between the underwear or in any pocket of his clothing. Pierce rifled through the bills and correspondence neatly filed in a drawer of the small desk. Everything in the bedroom looked spic and span, as did the bathroom. Not finding a speck of dust anywhere, not even a dust bunny under the bed, corroborated Miller's statement of Mr. Rudolph's proclivity for tidiness.

Miller sat on the couch looking sad, holding a knickknack in one hand and a newspaper page in the other. He dropped the items on the couch and stood when Pierce entered the room and spoke.

"I'll be off now, Mr. Miller. Thank you for letting me in to see the apartment. If you think of anything else, call my office, and please remember to call me Howard if we bump into each other while I'm here. We're supposed to be old friends."

"Yes. I'm sorry I called you Mr. Pierce before," Miller said.

"It's all right, but call me Howard, even on the phone. That way, you'll get used to it."

"I will."

"This may take a while, and in the end, I can't promise I'll be able to prove a homicide, but I'm going to give it my all, Mr. Miller."

"Thank you."

"Goodbye, sir."

6

*B*ack in the lobby, Pierce glanced at his watch. He'd been meeting with Wane Miller for an hour and had time to do a little exploring before Monica's shift ended. Casually walking around, he took in the sparkling chandeliers and the oil paintings on the wall. In the sitting area, people relaxed on cushioned chairs reading, conversing, or watching the news on the flat screen. Passing by the unisex salon, he noticed women getting their hair done or men having a shave or a haircut filling every seat. He read the Fitness Center, Ballroom and Theater signs on their respective doors as he walked by. At the restaurant, the menu posted on the window made his mouth water. *This place has everything. Must cost an arm and a leg to live here.*

A man carrying a carafe spotted Pierce when he stopped to take a peek inside the coffee room. Pierce recognized him as the same man who had conducted the exercise class at the pool.

He served a woman her cup of coffee and approached. "May I help you?" he asked, keys jangling from a chain attached to his belt.

"No, thank you. Just looking around."

"Thinking of moving here?"

"Perhaps," Pierce said, noncommittally.

"I'd be happy to show you around. If you have questions, I'm sure I'll have the answers," he said with confidence.

"No, thank you. I've already seen enough, but thank you for the offer."

"Well, if you decide to move in here, this is a wonderful place to live. I'm Mace Leyton, the handyman," he said, reaching for a handshake.

So this is Mace.

They shook hands. "Handyman? Weren't you holding a water exercise class earlier? I thought you were the swim instructor," Pierce said.

Mace smiled broadly, smoothing out the rough edges of his otherwise rugged face. "Well, I do pretty much about everything around here," he bragged.

"Such as?"

"I fix all kinds of small appliances for sure, but ..." He counted on his fingers, "I also solve computer problems, clean the swimming pool, vacuum, wipe down the counters, set up board games, lock up equipment for the night, make the coffee, and take care of anything else that needs doing. A bona fide jack of all trades."

If he'd been a rooster, he'd be crowing, Pierce thought.

"That's why you carry so many keys?"

Mace self-consciously grabbed the chain as if to protect it, a gesture not lost on Pierce.

The handyman leaned in and smiled. He put his open hand to the side of his mouth, and whispered, "I can't very well run up to Management every time I want to get some equipment, supplies, or service the pool, now can I?"

Pierce said, "Bet the residents consider you indispensable."

Mace's smile drooped a little at the corners, and his eyes narrowed.

Why the face? I was being friendly, thought Pierce.

"Oh, I don't know about that, but I'm happy to help where I can."

Wanting to catch Monica, Pierce said, "Nice to meet you," and left Mace with a bewildered look on his face.

Walking toward reception, Pierce swore he felt eyes on the back of his head.

Monica was on the phone. "Yes, that would be Thursday morning for the pickup. Goodbye." She hung up and looked at Pierce. "Hello again."

"Hello, Monica."

"How was your visit with Mr. Miller?"

"Fine," Pierce answered.

The phone rang. "Excuse me," she said.

Monica picked up. "One moment, please." After transferring the call, she again turned to Pierce. "Sorry about that."

"No need to apologize, Monica. I know I'm interrupting your work, but I promise to get out of your hair soon."

She smiled. "If you don't mind the interruptions, I'm happy to answer your questions."

"I'll be brief. Tell me, how many security guards work here?"

"Two. Frank and Josephine."

"What hours do they work?"

"Frank works from four in the afternoon until midnight. Josephine then starts at midnight until eight in the morning."

"So between the hours of eight and four, there's no security guard here?"

"No need. My shift starts at eight. If anything happens before Frank arrives, I will call 911. I've been working here for the past year and a half and never had a reason to call in an emergency. This is a pretty safe place."

"So on the morning Mr. Rudolph died, it wasn't you who called the police?"

"No. I wasn't in yet."

"Any idea who made that call?"

"Probably Josephine, but anyone could've called in the emergency."

"In the time you've worked here, have you witnessed any serious arguments or fights break out between the residents?"

"Not really," she said. "I mean, sure, people may argue over a game or politics, or maybe a movie they're watching, but I don't think these people get into fistfights." She chuckled at the thought of seeing old people punching one another.

"I see. What about petty theft? Has anyone ever accused someone of stealing?"

A couple, dressed in tennis clothes, came in. Monica greeted them. "Hello, Mr. and Mrs. Montgomery. Good game?"

"Yes, we won!" they said in unison, holding up their rackets as trophies, as they headed toward the elevator.

Monica turned to Pierce. "Stealing? No. Never. As you see from where they live, these people are well off. I don't think they would steal from one another."

You'd be surprised.

"Is there a lost and found here?"

"Yes. if someone loses something like a pair of glasses, it usually turns up in the lost and found, but you'll have to ask Mace about that."

"Mace, the handyman?"

"Yes. Have you met him?"

"I've had the pleasure."

"He's always willing to help everyone, no matter the problem. Changed a flat for me once."

Pierce shifted his weight from one foot to the other to alleviate the ache he sometimes felt when he stood too long because of an old injury to his back sustained during a tussle with a perpetrator trying to get away. That guy was a beast, throwing Pierce against a wall. It took three police officers to put him down.

"I'm sorry I don't have a chair for you," Monica said, noticing his discomfort.

"That's fine. I'm almost done. When you came in on the morning of Mr. Rudolph's death, did Josephine hang around for a while?"

"Just for a bit to fill me in on all the commotion still going on after they took Mr. Rudolph away."

"One more thing. Do employees clock in or sign your book when reporting for work?"

"Not this book. This is only for visitors. When we come in, we sign a timesheet and whoever is on duty has to initial the time. The security guards and I initial our signatures for one another and do the same for whoever signs in or out when we're on duty."

"Who keeps the timesheet?"

She pointed her hand to a small drawer in her desk. "It's kept in here. At the end of the week, I turn it over to the management office, and they give me a fresh sheet for the following week."

"If there's no one at the desk when an employee comes in, do they have access to the timesheet?"

"It's unusual for anyone to leave this post when employees report for work or at the end of their workday, but if there's no one here, they have to wait because, as I said, we keep the sheet locked in the drawer. If we don't sign it, we don't get paid."

"I see," Pierce said, wishing he could ask her for a peek.

"Why are you interested in how we sign in," she asked with a worried look.

Pierce lied. "My daughter is interested in starting a printing business with a few employees and she wondered how to keep track of their hours. Seeing your visitor's book reminded me."

"Signing in takes no time at all, but tell her she needs someone she can trust to make sure no one is cheating by adding extra hours."

"Thank you. I'll pass that on to her, and thanks for answering my questions, Monica."

"You're welcome."

Pierce was about to leave when she asked, "Do you think someone harmed Mr. Rudolph?"

"Not at all, Monica. I'm trying to get answers to ease Mr. Miller's mind. Perhaps I'll be back and try to talk to a few of the residents if he's still worried. I'd appreciate it if you didn't tell anyone of Mr. Miller's concerns. It wouldn't do to upset people unnecessarily."

"No, of course not. She touched her lips with her index finger. "Mum's the word."

Pierce was about to say goodbye when Monica waved to a man who entered the lobby. She cocked her head in his direction and said, "That's Frank, the security guard."

Pierced followed her gaze. Frank waved back at Monica with a friendly smile.

When he passed by Pierce, Frank looked at him with what Pierce thought was the habitual way law enforcement officers recognized one of their own. Pierce nodded, acknowledging the familiarity.

"Well, goodbye, Monica."

Pierce left with a head full of puzzle pieces waiting to be put together.

7

_____

*T*hings hadn't always worked out for Mace Leyton. Before getting the handyman position, he'd had a long work history of various minimum-wage jobs, never making enough money to afford much of anything. An unhappy and rebellious young man, he got fired more times than he could count, until he found himself homeless which led to his stealing food from a supermarket. That incident resulted in a two-year probation for the misdemeanor charge. After that, he roamed from one place to another until he landed at Coral Bells, tired of the street life.

The previous handyman had unexpectedly quit and after weeks of advertising for the position, no one had applied. When Mace Leyton walked in looking for work, Management was desperate to hire someone to keep the tenants happy. They were already complaining no one was tending to their needs. Mace's friendly grin on an otherwise menacing-looking face, fast talk, and fake written testimonials from businesses no longer in existence, got him hired.

On his first day on the job, Mace Leyton had unnerved more than a few residents when he introduced himself as their new handyman. His appearance, standing six feet three inches tall, weighing two hundred ten pounds of pure muscle, certainly didn't help allay their apprehension.

However, Mace's eagerness to work hard soon won him the trust of staff and residents alike, making sure anything asked of him, he did—sweeping floors, throwing out the trash, cleaning countertops, or keeping lonely residents company by reading to them or joining them for a game of cards. He read medication labels for one resident in particular who had trouble making out the small print. He smiled when a single woman at the apartments caught his eye, vying for his attention, but he never acted on coquetry.

During the week, Mace ran exercise and water aerobics lessons he learned from watching videos on his VCR. When someone asked him if he could repair a sewing machine, he assured the lady he would have it back to her good as new, despite knowing nothing about sewing machines. True to his word, he visited Pocono Sew & Vac, explained the problem, and left the store with the proper parts and know-how he needed to repair the machine. Mace was a quick learner. With his first paycheck, he bought some do-it-yourself books and videos after paying rent for a one-bedroom walkup near enough to the complex that he could walk to work. There was nothing he wouldn't do to keep the best job he ever had.

After six months, Mace Leyton had become a fixture, well acquainted with everyone's routine, leaving him the full, unimpeded run of the place.

Suspicious by nature, Mace did not think the man casually walking around the property fit the description of someone who could afford to live at a swanky place like Coral Bells. He'd been around affluent people long enough to tell the difference between the haves, the have-nots, and the pretenders.

Why is this out-of-place man chatting up Monica for so long? If he wanted information about this place, why ask the receptionist? he wondered. It bothered Mace he'd offered to show the stranger around and answer all of his questions, but he preferred to talk to Monica. *Doesn't make sense… unless he's flirting.* Mace discarded that notion when he studied Pierce's body language. Although friendly, his demeanor did not suggest any personal interest in the attractive receptionist. The more he thought about it, the more he wanted to find out what that man was doing at Coral Bells. Perhaps Monica would shed some light on this mystery person.

Mace barely had time to mop up a spill in the game room before hurrying to reception, hoping to catch Monica. Frank sat at the desk when he got there. He caught a glimpse of her ready to walk out the front door and quickened his pace to catch up to her.

Frank called out, "Monica, you forgot your shades." She came back and reached out to grab the sunglasses from Frank's outstretched hand. "Thanks, Frank. I had a feeling I forgot something, but I'm sure I would've remembered as soon as that bright sun blinded me," she chuckled.

"Glad to be of service," Frank said. "Have a good evening. *Again.*"

"Yes, you too. *Again.*"

While this went on, Mace walked past them and out the door to wait for Monica.

When she stepped outside, he accosted her. "Hey Monica, let me walk you to your car. I want to ask you something."

Monica hesitated, hoping Mace didn't intend to ask her for a date. Most men gravitated to her ever since developing a woman's curvy figure at the tender age of twelve. With her creamy chocolate skin and hazel eyes, men found her captivating. Although Mace had never made a move on her, she thought he was probably biding his time. But Monica wasn't interested in Mace and desperately tried to think of a reason to turn him down.

Wary, she asked, "What is it, Mace?"

Catching the oh-shit look on her face, Mace donned his friendliest smile to put her at ease. "No big deal, Monica. Just me being curious."

"Curious about what, Mace?" she said, sounding snotty.

"Was that man standing by your desk looking to buy in here?"

Monica almost breathed a sigh of relief but caught herself. "What? Why do you ask?"

"I wanted to ask him if he needed any help when I saw him wandering around earlier, although I thought he didn't quite fit the profile of someone who could afford to live here."

When she narrowed her eyes, he added, "I got busy, so I never got the chance. Anyhow, I just wanted to make sure he wasn't bothering you."

Mace had never shown an interest in prospective buyers or ever questioned her when someone stood by her desk to talk. She didn't quite buy his explanation, not that she ever had a reason to be suspicious of Mace. Still, she found his curiosity odd. "No, he wasn't bothering me," she said. "I think he's interested in buying here and asked a lot of questions."

"Like what?"

"Ah, you know, Mace. Usual questions people ask when they're looking for a place to live."

"He doesn't look rich enough to afford this place," Mace said.

"Well, you can't tell who's rich by their appearance, Mace. Look at Mr. Martinez. He goes around in a tee shirt and jeans most of the time, and he's loaded."

"Of course, you're right, Monica. Just a feeling I got is all." He tried to look sheepish.

"Yeah, well, you can't judge a book by its cover, is all I'm saying," said Monica.

"It was just a feeling, but I see your point."

"Gotta go, Mace," she said, wanting to end the conversation before she inadvertently shared Mr. Miller's concerns.

"Okay, bye now."

"Bye, Mace."

Mace watched her until she had driven away.

She's hiding something.

"Hey, Mace," Frank greeted when he went back inside.

Deep in thought, Mace did not hear him. Frank tried again. "Yo, Mace."

Frank's voice broke his contemplation. "Oh, hi, Frank."

"Must be something important that got you thinking so hard."

Years of experience had taught Mace to lie easily. "Just trying to work out a problem with the generator, that's all."

"Is the generator not working?"

"It's working, but not as it should. Don't worry, I'll have it fixed in no time. Already got it figured out."

"That's why you're the handyman," Frank said with a smile.

The phone rang. "See you, Mace. Better get to fixing the generator."

"Yes, See you, Frank."

8

After his brief conversation with Monica, Pierce drove directly to the hospital. He rode the elevator to the lowest level and went through the double doors into the morgue. Bent over her desk filling out forms, sat Lucy Strunk, the diener. She looked up when Pierce entered the small office. "Hey, Detective Pierce," she said. "What brings you here? I thought you retired."

"I did, but in my second life, I'm doing private investigations."

She propped her elbow on her desk and put her fist under her chin. "You don't say?"

"You know what they say."

"Yeah, yeah."

"Once a cop always a cop," they chanted, laughing.

"How are you, Lucy?"

"Me? Shoot, I'm always good."

"Glad to hear it."

"Well then, how can I help you, Private Investigator Pierce?" Lucy said, sitting back.

"I need some information on a body that was brought in yesterday, name of Wane Rudolph."

"Why the interest?"

"Someone close to the decedent doesn't buy cause of death. Thinks his friend was murdered."

"All due respect, but since you're no longer working Homicide, why are you investigating?"

"Sergeant Ramirez asked me to look into it."

"Oh, well, if Iggy sent you, I'm happy to oblige," she said, chuckling and picking up a pile of neatly stacked papers on her desk. When she found Wane Rudolph's paperwork, she adjusted her glasses higher on her nose and perused the file. "Yes, says here he died of natural causes." She raised an eyebrow. "Let me guess, you think otherwise."

Pierce said. "Perhaps. TOD?"

Lucy again referred to the report. "The coroner logged the time of death at 7:50 a.m." She lowered her glasses and peered over them. " But you know, of course, that's when he examined the body after arriving at the scene and calling it. The M.E. determined death occurred sometime between 5:30 and 7:30 a.m."

"I understand," said Pierce.

She put down the report and took off her glasses. "Follow me."

The morgue assistant walked out of her office and down the corridor to the refrigerated room. She went around two of the bodies on gurneys and stopped in front of the third. "This is Mr. Rudolph."

"Thanks, Lucy."

"Take your time. I have work to do," she said and walked out.

Pierce pulled down the sheet to uncover Mr. Rudolph's face. There were deep, scarlet tracks around the bridge of his nose, chin, and mouth.

Those marks look raw. According to Miller, Rudolph hated the CPAP. He wouldn't have fit the mask on his face so tight as to leave impressions such as these. Otherwise, how could he have fallen asleep comfortably? thought Pierce.

He uncovered the rest of the body and examined his hands and underneath his fingernails, looking for signs of a struggle, but found none. He pulled up the sheet and left Mr. Rudolph as he'd found him.

Entering her office again, Pierce asked, "Lucy, what does the M.E. say about the bruises on Mr. Rudolph's face?"

She again picked up the file and stretched her arm out to hand it to Pierce. "Third paragraph, page two, pathologist report," she said.

Pierce grabbed the file and went through it until he found the form. They attributed the marks to a tight CPAP mask improperly fitted onto the decedent's face. Pierce nodded.

He continued reading. 'No other trauma to the body.'

Pierce gave the report back to Lucy. "Can you print a photograph of Mr. Rudolph's face?"

Lucy put down her pen. "Sure." She clicked an icon on her computer. When she located the folder, she clicked on the photo and sent it to the printer.

"I'm off," said Pierce. "Thanks for letting me examine the body. I'm sorry I interrupted your work."

She smiled. "Happy to help, detective, I mean, private eye." She grinned. "It was nice to see you. Don't forget to grab your photo from the printer."

"Yes. Thanks again, Lucy. Nice seeing you too."

"Bye, Pierce," she said and went back to filling out forms.

"Bye, Lucy." Pierce grabbed the photo and left the morgue.

Back at the office, he spent the next hour researching CPAP machines and how to wear the masks properly. They're supposed to fit snugly but not so tight they leave marks such as the ones on Mr. Rudolph's face.

He closed the web pages and sat back in his chair, trying to come up with a plausible alternative reason for the condition of Mr. Rudolph's face. He could think of none. Those marks confirmed to Pierce he had a homicide on his hands. Otherwise, a person would have to be impervious to pain to wear a mask that tight.

In the end, the only thing that made sense is that someone held Mr. Rudolph down by putting pressure on his mask until Mr. Rudolph had a heart attack and died. It had to have been someone strong enough to hold down a panicked man.

———

THE NEXT MORNING, Pierce got up early and casually ate his breakfast while going over what he had learned. He intended to go back to Coral Bells, this time as a prospective buyer. That handyman was already suspicious of him.

Louise interrupted his thinking. "You look pensive, Howie."

"Oh, sorry. Were you saying something?"

"Just goodbye. I have an appointment at the hairdresser."

"What for? You already look beautiful."

"Flatterer!" She leaned down and kissed him. "See you tonight. Have a nice day."

"You too, hon."

Pierce looked at his watch. *Ruby should be in by now.*

In the den, he called his office.

"Morning Ruby."

"Morning, boss."

"Ruby, I want you to see if you can get me an appointment to tour the Coral Bells Adult Living apartments."

"For when?"

"Try to get me in this morning. I'm going to serve those warrants. Should be done by ten. Any time after that is fine."

"You have an appointment with Mrs. Lebron at eleven."

"Please postpone that for me, will ya?"

"Okay. I'll call you back."

"Thanks."

Ten minutes later, Ruby called. "You're to see a Miss Inez Santos at eleven thirty this morning for a tour."

"You're a peach, Ruby."

"Don't I know it?" she said and hung up.

Dressed in his business suit, Pierce drove off in search of the two people he had to serve. He stood in front of the building where the man involved in a child custody battle worked. Ten minutes later, he saw him rushing toward the front door with a bag strapped around his shoulder, a newspaper under his arm and holding a cup of coffee. Pierce stopped him before he went through. "Excuse me, Mr. David Brown?"

"Yes," he answered automatically, thinking this person was his nine-thirty interviewee, arriving early.

Identity confirmed, Pierce reached into his briefcase and pulled out the envelope containing the warrant. He offered it to Mr. Brown. The man gave him a curious look but accepted the envelope. Pierce said, "You've been served," leaving Mr. Brown with a surprised expression on his face.

Should've expected it. You ignored a subpoena.

The other person took more time to locate. He was not at either of the two addresses Pierce had for him, and he worried he was going to be late for his appointment with Miss Santos. At times like these, Pierce lamented not having an associate to take care of tasks such as serving warrants.

It took a bit of legwork asking around as to his whereabouts, but Pierce finally found him, sitting at a bar. He approached, and again simply asked his name. The man, who owed more parking tickets than a diplomat, accepted the envelope.

Pierce went on his way, shaking his head.

He made it to Coral Bells twenty minutes after eleven, glad Ruby hadn't made the appointment earlier or he would have been late. *What would I do without Ruby keeping things running smoothly?*

Monica smiled when she saw him. "Hello again."

"Hi, Monica."

She motioned for Pierce to bend towards her and whispered, "When I left yesterday, Mace was waiting for me outside. I thought he was going to ask me for a date," she scoffed, "but that wasn't it."

"Pierce asked, What did he want?"

"Excuse me." Monica turned and answered the ringing telephone. "Coral Bells."

When she transferred the call, she again motioned for Pierce to bend toward her. "Mace asked me if you were looking to move in here."

"He did?"

"Yes. I told him you're thinking about it. Asked if you had a lot of questions. I said yes, questions people ask when looking for an apartment, but I don't think he believed me. Then I remembered what you said and cut the conversation short."

"Thank you, Monica. You handled that exactly right."

She grinned. "You can count on me, Mr. Martal."

"I appreciate that, Monica. Anything else?"

"Not really. He's never asked about anyone wanting information from me. After all, I *am* the receptionist. People ask me questions all the time."

"Perhaps I hurt his feelings when I turned down his offer to show me around," Pierce said.

"What?" she asked, stunned. "He offered to show you around?"

"Yes."

"He didn't tell me *that*. Mace said he thought about it but got busy."

"Don't worry about it. As I said, his feelings were probably hurt," Pierce said.

Pressing her lips together, Monica thought about that and reluctantly agreed. "Yeah, that must be it."

"I'm sure it was jealousy or curiosity on his part. Nothing to worry about."

"If you say so."

"Now, on what floor is the management office?"

"Seventh floor."

Pierce signed the log and said, "See you later."

———

INEZ SANTOS, responsible for selling units, enthusiastically led Pierce around the grounds. He nodded his head in appreciation every time she proudly showed off residents enjoying the amenities. "This is a regulation-size professional swimming pool," she boasted when they passed by. Pierce swam professionally when he competed in college and knew she exaggerated.

"Do you like to play bocce ball, Mr. Martal?" she asked.

"Never played, but it looks like fun," he answered, aware bocce ball was not likely to be in his future.

"Yes, residents love it. They've formed teams to compete against one another. How about shuffleboard?" she asked, barely taking a breath.

"Sure, I probably would enjoy that." *Not.*

"Good. Let's head inside. I have lots to show you."

After being in the ninety-degree sun, the cool air, although welcomed, gave him chills. His shirt stuck to his back, and his temples glistened with perspiration.

The sales representative seemed cool as a cucumber in her short-sleeved white cotton shirt, name tag prominently placed above the breast pocket etched in gold lettering, 'Inez Santos, Coral Bells Adult Living.' Her baby blue colored skirt fell just above her knees showing off her long, tan legs, down to her white ankle socks and tennis shoes.

A tour of the hair salon, movie theater, ball room and fitness center followed. Pierce barely listened to her sales pitch, scanning the faces of residents milling about, taking notice of their demeanors if their eyes met his.

When Mace bumped into them on the main floor, Pierce acknowledged him with a nod.

"Hello again," he said. The saleswoman cut her eyes in Mace's direction, not appreciating the intrusion.

"Hello, Mace," Pierce said.

"You've come back for the tour, I see."

"Yes. I thought about what you said yesterday and came back for a second look."

Mace grinned from ear to ear. "Glad you did."

Miss Santos looked at her watch, annoyance written all over her face. "If you don't mind, Mace, I'd like to continue my tour."

Mace gave her an exaggerated bow. "Yes, of course, Miss Inez." He turned to Pierce. "As I mentioned yesterday, this is a great place to live. I hope Miss Inez will convince you."

"This way, sir," Miss Santos said, motioning for Pierce to follow her. Pierce nodded his goodbye to Mace, who stared after them.

The saleswoman continued reciting her rehearsed script. "Unlike other facilities of this kind, we have a restaurant many have rated five stars. The chef came to us from a prestigious eatery in New York City. We're lucky to have him. Come, I've arranged for us to have lunch."

Like the rest of the building, they decorated the restaurant with gleaming chandeliers. The tables, dressed in white linen with fine silverware placed beside cloth napkins, were adorned with colorful centerpieces of freshly cut flowers.

Pierce's stomach gurgled when he breathed in the aromatic scent circulating throughout the dining room. Following Miss

Santos to their table, he turned his head from side to side, admiring the tantalizing-looking meals at the diners' tables.

They sure know how to pour it on.

The waiter brought them menus as soon as the maître d' seated them.

"Would you like something to drink, Mr. Martal?" the saleswoman asked.

"Water's fine."

"Sparkling or regular?"

"Regular water, please."

"How about a glass of wine with your dinner?"

Pierce never drank alcohol on a job unless he couldn't avoid it to get the information he sought.

"No, thank you."

She was disappointed he had declined the wine, a treat she allowed herself to enjoy only when visiting the company restaurant with a prospective buyer. The daughter of an alcoholic, she did not trust herself to follow in her father's footsteps. If he'd asked for wine or a cocktail, she would have joined him.

Miss Santos said to the waiter who had been standing nearby, "Water for us both, please." She turned her attention to Pierce. "What do you think so far, Mr. Martal?"

"I like it very much."

"Excellent. When we're done here, I'll show you an empty apartment we still have available."

"All right."

"Now please, order whatever you like. It's on us."

"Thank you."

Pierce read the menu, which had no prices listed, but since he did not have to pay, he ordered the porterhouse with mushrooms and fingerling potatoes, and a Caesar salad.

I should call Louise and tell her not to save dinner for me.

Miss Santos ordered the same and kept up the sales talk in between bites of steak. Pierce tuned her out, trying to enjoy the delicious fare in front of him while checking out the room. Every so often, he would nod politely, as if interested in her chatter.

Pierce noticed people were staring at his table. A woman openly gave him the eye. Pierce smiled, establishing a friendly connection should he later have occasion to question her.

When they finished their meal, Miss Santos asked, "Do you have questions?"

Pierce turned his attention back to her. "Yes, how is security around here?"

"This is a safe place, I assure you. There's never been an incident serious enough to call the police since I've worked here."

"From what agency do you hire security guards?"

In all the years she'd been selling apartments at Coral Bells, no one had ever asked her to name the agency where they hired security guards. Searching her memory, she said, "I believe they're hired from an agency called Closed Doors." She smiled, congratulating herself for coming up with the answer so quickly.

"Clever name."

"Yes," she agreed. "But we have never had cause to tighten security." She wanted to get off the security topic, and blurted, "The chef makes a wonderful crème brûlée. Shall we order dessert?"

"No, thank you. I couldn't eat another bite."

He could see her disappointment. "But you order dessert for yourself."

"Oh no, I'm stuffed too," she said and signaled the waiter. "Please ask the chef to come by."

He bowed and disappeared through the traffic doors. A minute later, a tall and beefy man, clad in a typical short bib apron, necktie, checkered pants, and a toque Blanche on his head, filled the room with his presence. Like a rock star aware of everyone's eyes on him, he walked directly to Pierce's table, ignoring his admirers.

Pierce stared at the imposing man standing before him.

"May I present Chef Grant Delacroix?" said the saleswoman. "Chef, this is Mr. Howard Martal."

Delacroix smiled and extended his hand. Pierce pushed back his chair and stood, holding onto his napkin. He thought his grip felt a bit too heavy-handed for a chef.

"That's a powerful grip you have there, chef."

A laugh, as potent as he looked, came out of the chef's mouth. "I used to play football in my younger days, but I still like to keep in shape when I'm not cooking."

Pierce caught a whiff of mint when he spoke.

"Oh yeah? What position?"

"Linebacker."

"Impressive."

Delacroix laughed again. "Yeah, I had the body for it."

"Thank you for the delicious meal," Pierce said.

"It's my pleasure. I'm glad you enjoyed it."

"Mr. Martal is considering a move to Coral Bells," Santos said.

"You won't find a better place to live. I hope you'll be dining with us again soon."

"Thank you," Pierce said.

"Gotta get back to the kitchen. Nice to have met you."

As quickly as he had marched over, he disappeared through the traffic doors.

Miss Santos pushed back her chair and stood. "How about I show you one of our units?"

Although he had already seen Millers' and Rudolph's apartments, Pierce had no choice but to play along. "Lead the way," he said.

On the second floor, the rep unlocked the door to an empty apartment and ushered Pierce in. "This is our two-bedroom suite," she said.

"As I told you before you started the tour, I have no wife or children. Two bedrooms are more than I need," Pearce said, wanting to end the tour.

"Yes, I'm sorry. Unfortunately, there are no one-bedrooms available at the moment."

"You might have mentioned that earlier," Pierce said, realizing he sounded annoyed, which on second thought, he assumed is how a wealthy person would react when not getting his way.

A bit flustered, she put on her best smile and said, "I didn't want you to leave without showing you how nice the bigger units are. Come, let me show you the layout. It has a wonderful view of the property. You'll see why the apartments on this side of the building are the most popular suites."

"You're not listening to me," Pierce insisted.

Sensing she was about to lose her commission, she turned and asked, "What kind of work do you do, Mr. Martal?"

Pierce elaborated on what he had told Monica, and with a tinge of arrogance, said, "I run the science department at ESU," a lie he felt certain she would not waste her time verifying.

She perked up. "Well, the extra bedroom might serve as an office or a library," a place to keep all those books and papers I'm sure you have."

"I have an office at the university where I keep all that. An office or library where I live would remain empty, a waste of space. Thank you for showing me around." He turned and reached for the doorknob, eager to get to the real purpose of his interest in Coral Bells.

Miss Santos' strategy had always been to show the two bedrooms first, earning a bigger sales commission. If that failed, she would then offer to show the smaller units. But this time, no one-bedroom apartment was available. Desperately trying to cinch the deal, she blurted what she never revealed in her sales pitch lest people go for the smaller unit. "The layout for the two-bedroom suite is the same as the single bedroom." She hoped she did not sound desperate.

Although Pierce had inspected Mr. Rudolph's one-bedroom apartment, perhaps he would learn something new from Miss Santos. Turning around, he asked, "It is?"

Thinking she might still pull off this sale, she eagerly said, "Yes, all units are designed the same way, even the studios minus the bedrooms, of course."

Remembering what Mr. Miller had told him about the wet floor, he looked down. "Do all the apartments have ceramic tiled floors?" he asked, not sure if the material of the floor had any significance.

"Oh goodness, no. The floors are not ceramic. Don't want our residents to slip and hurt themselves on ceramic floors. These are the finest vinyl tiles on the market. They look like ceramic, but they're not," she said, happy to be in selling mode again. "Come, let me walk you through the unit."

"All right."

Not learning anything new after the tour, except the floors are not ceramic tile, Pierce promised he would give the apartment thoughtful consideration.

"Don't wait too long. These units sell fast," Miss Santos said.

"I won't. Thank you for showing me around, Miss Santos. I'll call you soon."

The saleswoman walked away, certain she had lost the sale.

9

$\mathcal{E}$xiting the elevator in the lobby, Pierce heard someone call out, *"Yoo-hoo, Yoo-hoo!"*

He turned toward the voice. A woman dressed in long white pants and a sleeveless, sun-yellow top, dashed across the lobby in her gold, slingback shoes, her silver hair tied in a ponytail, swinging back and forth. She held down a colorful beaded necklace against her chest with a perfectly manicured hand.

Pierce recognized her as one of the restaurant diners who had been staring at his table. With painted red lips and cheeks, and gold eyeshadow, she had a face not easily forgettable.

Reaching him, she gushed out, "I was at the restaurant earlier when you were dining with our salesperson. Inez does an excellent job, but if you're looking to move in, there's no one better than me to fill you in on the real nitty-gritty of what it's like to live here."

Amused, Pierce said, "You don't say?"

"Oh yes," she said, casually touching his arm. "You've had the VIP tour, but I know the answers to the questions that matter. Ask me anything about the people, the services, anything."

Pierce smiled. "Thank you, Miss?"

"Grace Johnson, at your service." She held out her delicate hand which did not look sturdy enough for her large diamond rings.

"Nice to meet you, Miss Johnson," Pierce said, shaking her hand.

"Please, call me Grace. And you are?"

"Howard Martal."

Grace smiled and took him by the arm as if they were old friends. "Come, Howard, let's grab a cup of coffee and have a chat."

When they were comfortably seated in the coffee room, Grace tilted her head in the direction of a couple who had just walked in. "See those two over there?" she said, lowering her voice, "They're having an affair, well, she is. He's a widower, but she's still married. Can't say I blame her, though. Her husband is an arrogant SOB if you pardon my French."

Pierce smiled politely.

A tall and thin man, who had been sitting by himself, rose to leave. Grace turned her attention toward him. "That one," she said, again tilting her head, "showing off his skinny legs in those short shorts, he's never been married. According to him, ladies consider him quite a catch. Struts around here like a Don Juan, and even though he's lost his good looks if he ever had any," she smirked, "not to mention his hair, he still behaves like a bon vivant and womanizer par excellence," she said in an exaggerated French accent. "I'm kinda sorry for the guy."

Pierce took a sip of coffee and asked, "Been living here long, Miss Johnson?"

She blew on her coffee and also took a sip. "Since 2001, and it's Grace, remember?"

"Grace."

"My husband, Danny, and I moved in a little over seven years ago. He passed away a couple of years later," she said sadly.

"My condolences."

"Thank you. Anyway, we'd made a few friends here. After Danny died, some neighbors came by to see if I needed anything. They invited me to join them for a meal, trying to get me out of my apartment to keep me from dwelling on my loss. Little by little, I warmed up to these kind people. There isn't a tenant in this whole complex I have not met." She sat straighter, and with a wide grin, said, "Everyone calls me the mayor because I go around greeting newcomers."

"Did you welcome Mr. Rudolph when he moved in, Grace?"

"Yes, of course. Poor man. He didn't participate in the activities I'm interested in, so we didn't often run into each other, but I got to talk to him in cooking class."

"What did you talk about?"

"Oh, you know, the usual things. Life at Coral Bells, cooking, the weather, yadda, yadda. I was looking forward to the dinner party he was throwing, to demonstrate his cooking skills I imagine." She shook her head. "It's a shame he never got to show off. From what I observed in class, he was doing quite well."

"My friend, Jenaro Miller, talked him into taking that class."

"Oh yes, Jenaro. You know him?"

"Yes. He's the one who recommended I move here."

"Is that right? Small world."

"Other than yourself, did Mr. Rudolph have any other friends he liked to talk to?" Pierce asked.

Grace gave him an odd look, and said, "Mr. Miller was his best friend. You saw Wane Rudolph, you saw Jenaro Miller. Two peas in a pod they were. I never saw Wane having a long conversation with anyone else. Why do you ask?"

"No reason. I've known Jenaro for a while. Nice man, but when it came to his friendship with Mr. Rudolph, he seemed overly protective of him."

"That's the way it is with best friends. Me? I have many friends, and I don't play favorites," she said proudly.

Pierce again smiled. "I do worry about Jenaro though, Grace. Now that Mr. Rudolph has passed away, he seems lost. I thought perhaps if Mr. Rudolph had befriended someone else, Jenaro might gravitate to that person, as a sort of stand-in for his departed friend."

"Hmm. I seriously doubt you can replace a best friend so easily, Howard."

"Yeah. You're probably right, Grace."

Pierce took a sip of coffee before asking the chatty Miss Johnson his next question. "You said you know the nitty-gritty around here. Any unpleasant people live or work here?"

Grace seemed to puff up like a balloon whose air was ready to escape. "I'll say. Let's see. There's Mr. Jackson in Apartment 502. He's always in a bad mood."

"Has Mr. Jackson ever had occasion to argue with Mr. Rudolph, that you're aware of?"

"No, he doesn't argue, just goes around with his nose in the air, barely speaking to anyone. If someone does speak to him, he rebuffs them." She reached across the table and touched Pierce's hand. "You don't suppose, he's shy and that's why he doesn't speak to anyone? Do you?"

"That's possible, Grace."

"Funny how I never thought about that until now," she said, pulling her hand away.

Pierce knew he was pushing it, but took a chance. "I understand Mr. Rudolph took over the bible studies class. Any conflict there?"

Grace creased her eyebrows. "Why all this interest in Mr. Rudolph?"

Shit.

Pierce leaned forward and lowered his voice. "Can I confide in you, Grace?"

Grace's eyes almost popped out of her sockets, making her

face look more clownish than it already did. She leaned in, anticipating a juicy piece of gossip.

"Jenaro is having difficulty accepting the death of his friend. He figured since I'm looking the place over before deciding to move in, I might hear something. Despite my better judgment, I told him I'd keep my ears open."

"Oh my. Does he think Mr. Rudolph was murdered?" Grace asked, relishing the possibility of an inside scoop.

Pierce repeated the familiar sentiment he used on Monica. "I doubt that very much, Grace. I think some people look for reasons when someone they love suddenly dies. I don't think there's anything to it. After all, the police did not find anything suspicious, and let's not forget, the coroner examined the body and ruled Mr. Rudolph's death as natural causes."

Grace sat back in her chair, not convinced. She stared at him for a moment before asking, "Who are you? Are you a policeman?"

Pierce laughed. "Nah, just a friend of Jenaro, doing him a favor."

Smart woman.

"So tell me about the bible studies class. Who runs it?"

Although somewhat skeptical, Grace relented. "The group was started by Jamie Alinsky a couple of years ago as soon as he moved here from the city."

"What city, Grace?"

She clicked her tongue. "Don't you know when people from New York say city, it means Manhattan?"

"Did you move here from New York, Grace?"

"Never lived there but I've been around New Yorkers long enough to have learned their lingo."

"I see. Where'd you come from before moving here?"

"Boston," she said, validating her accent.

"Nice town," Pierce said.

"And I would have stayed there but Danny liked the Poconos.

He and his dad used to come here to hunt every year when he was a kid. The place had fond memories for him, so we moved, and now I love it here too."

"Tell me, Grace, are you a member of the bible group?" Pierce asked wanting to get back on track.

"Me? Oh no. Never been one for organized religion. I worship privately. I don't like people telling me how I should interpret the bible, especially when a lot of those discussions lead to arguments. But I guess people just want to be heard. To each his own, as they say."

"So, you don't know much about what goes on in that group."

"I told you. I know the nitty-gritty of what happens around here. I'm the mayor, remember? Of course, I know all about that group," Grace said feigning hurt feelings.

"Sorry, Madam Mayor," Pierce said, looking contrite.

She bowed her head. "That's more like it."

"Is Mr. Alinsky still running the meetings?"

"He quit weeks ago when Mr. Rudolph pushed his way into the position, but I guess now that he's passed, Jamie will take it over again." Grace's eyes enlarged. "You don't suppose Jamie had anything to do with Wane's death, do you?"

Fuck me!

Pierce patiently explained as if talking to a child, "Grace, there is no evidence of foul play regarding the death of Mr. Rudolph. If there were, the police would have found it, don't you think?"

She shrugged her shoulders and reluctantly said, "I guess so."

"So why did Mr. Alinsky quit his group?" Pierce asked.

"I don't like speaking ill of the dead, you understand, but from the day Wane began attending the class, he argued constantly with Jamie on the meaning of one bible story or another. Sometimes it got so heated, Jamie would end the meeting. But that didn't stop Wane from arguing. He even won some members over to his side. I tell you, Jamie was forced out. It's a shame, too. Everyone likes him, as far as I can tell."

"Did others leave for the same reason as Mr. Alinsky?"

"Sure. When Jamie left, others followed. It had gotten intense between those two."

Pierce mentally added Jamie Alinsky's name to his list of people to investigate.

Even though Grace said she never attended, Pierce was impressed she knew so much about the class. "For someone who never participated, you seem very well-informed, Grace," he said.

She inhaled, blew out her breath slowly, and placed her hand over her heart, banging her ring against her necklace. "Mr. Martal," she said.

"Howard, please."

Putting on a serious face as if she were again offended, she said, "Howard, I'm a people person. Everyone confides in me even when I don't ask them to. They know I don't spread gossip. I may not go to bible studies, *Howard*, but the members are friends of mine who keep me up to date."

Pierce saw through her act but went along with it. "I apologize, Grace. I do believe what you're telling me and appreciate your trust in me. Please, go on."

"Aah, I know you didn't mean to offend me. Sometimes I can't resist ribbing someone I like." She again reached across the table and touched Howard's hand.

"Phew," Howard said, running his fingers across his forehead and flicking his hand. "I believed you were serious, Grace."

She giggled like a schoolgirl.

"Is there anything else you can tell me about that class, Grace?"

"That's all there is to it. Wane ran the class until his death. The group did not meet this week, obviously, but I hear the members asked Jamie to come back. If you move here, are you thinking of joining Jamie's group?"

"Me? No. I'm not interested in organized religion either."

Grace threw her head back and let out a hearty laugh. Pierce joined her.

"I knew I liked you for a reason, Howard," she said, almost choking.

Pierce drank the last of his coffee and sat back in his chair. "Tell me more about life at Coral Bells, Grace."

No sooner had Grace begun to describe the benefits of living at Coral Bells, than the handyman entered the room, ready to serve the usual residents, now coming in for a game of cards and a snack.

At first, Mace didn't see Pierce sitting with Miss Johnson. He headed straight to the coffee machine, but his ears perked up when he recognized that distinctive way of talking that got on his nerves—a scratchy voice with a Kennedy-sounding accent. It had to belong to the resident busybody, he thought. When he turned and saw the man Grace was so animatedly talking to, he found it suspicious that a man he had never before seen visiting, was acquainted with not only Monica and Mr. Miller but also with Grace Johnson.

Mace filled the coffee machine and casually walked over to their table.

"Hello again," he said, addressing Pierce.

Pierce had seen Mace when he first walked in and had kept a side eye on him. "Hello, Mace," Pierce said, bothered Mace found it necessary to approach him whenever he saw him.

"You two know each other?" asked Grace.

"We met yesterday," said Pierce.

"I offered to show him around, but he preferred the *professional* tour." Although Mace pronounced the word *professional*, with a smile, there was no mistaking the condescension in his voice.

"I'm sure you had more important things to do than to show me around, Mace," Pierce said.

Grace looked from one to the other, savoring the tension between the two.

"As Miss Grace will tell you, I'm always happy to help. Isn't that right, Miss Grace?"

"Oh yes. Mace is a treasure around here," she said sincerely.

"I'm sure he is," Pierce said, catching a slight tightening of Mace's smile.

"Can I freshen your coffees?" Mace said.

"No thanks," said Pierce.

"I'm good," said Grace, who had let her coffee get cold.

"Then I'll leave you to your conversation. Nice to see you again...uh..." He turned to Pierce. "I didn't catch your name yesterday."

"Martal, Howard Martal."

"Have a pleasant day, Mr. Martal."

"You too, Mace."

When Mace turned his back, Grace, asked, "What's going on between you two?"

"I'm afraid I hurt his feelings when I declined his kind offer to show me around. I already had an appointment with Miss Santos, or I would have gladly taken him up on it."

She raised an eyebrow. "Looked to me like there's more to it than that."

He laughed. "Nothing more than that, I assure you."

Pierce thought he'd better get back to asking pertinent questions someone looking to move in might ask.

"What makes this place special, Grace?"

"That's easy. Like I said before, it's the people. Although there are a few individuals I don't care for, most are friendly. And there's a lot to do here if you don't want to wallow alone in your apartment."

"What do you mean?"

"Well, take Mr. Anderson in Suite 308. The only time you see him is when he takes his walks around the complex. He doesn't belong to any club or partake in any of the activities, not even swimming, which is a terrific way to get in your exercise. I, myself, like to keep in shape by swimming, and playing tennis. The older you get, the more exercise you need," she said emphatically.

"That's true, but you said he walks every day, so maybe that's enough exercise for him."

Grace thought about it for a moment and laughed. "Funny how I've never considered walking to be exercise. Mr. Anderson walks every day, so that's something. The widow Peck in room 502 also prefers walking. Both of them are rather rude though, never bidding anyone a good day. Maybe they should get together."

Pierce was mentally taking note of the people Grace mentioned.

As if it never occurred to her before, Grace said, "You don't suppose the death of her husband ... or ... perhaps she'd been mistreated, is why Mrs. Peck stays away from people? And maybe Mr. Anderson has also suffered a loss. Everyone has a story you know," she said with certainty.

"Or they enjoy their own company," Pierce said.

"Maybe, but there's a limit to how much time you want to spend alone if you ask *me*."

"Belong to any clubs, Grace?"

"Oh heavens, no. Having to attend meetings or follow rules is not for me. I do things on my own time. When I'm not swimming or playing tennis with whoever is available, I enjoy dancing. We hold dances here every weekend. They're great fun and also a way to keep in shape, not to mention enjoying the company of men," she winked.

Pierce enjoyed Grace's enthusiasm and the way she criticized but then came up with a non-judgmental excuse for the people she had just disparaged. He spent a pleasant and informative two hours in her company.

When he left Grace, Pierce sat in his car and pulled his pad out of his pocket, lamenting the fact he was undercover. Taking notes in front of Grace would have fed her suspicions. He wrote the names of the people Grace had mentioned, and the particulars associated with their names.

Thanks to Grace, Pierce had enough information to kickstart his investigation.

10

While on the detective squad, Pierce rarely discussed his cases in great detail with his wife, but perhaps Louise might shed some light on the know-it-all handyman.

At the dinner table, Pierce said, "Hon, guess who called me today?"

"Who called you, Howie?" she said, passing him the salad dressing.

"Iggy," he said, grabbing the bottle and pouring the dressing on his salad.

"How is he?"

"He's good. Busy, but good."

Louise picked up her salad fork, stabbed at a slice of cucumber, and said, "What did he say?"

"He asked me to interview someone for him."

She took a bite, and asked the obvious question, "Does he need you to help him solve a homicide?"

"Uh-huh." Pierce picked up his glass of chardonnay and looked into Louise's almond-shaped, brown eyes. She smiled and lifted her glass to him. After they clinked glasses, they each took a sip, and Pierce said, "Thank you for making dinner. I didn't think I'd be hungry after that meal I had with the saleswoman at Coral Bells."

"Howie, you'd think you would know better after all those late nights when you were working Homicide. I've always made dinner in case you got home hungry."

"And that's another reason I love you so much."

"Go on now, tell me all about your conversation with Iggy."

"I will," he said, picking up the bowl of au gratin potatoes, "but first let me dig into this scrumptious dinner." He heaped a spoonful on his plate and reached for the green beans. Louise passed him the Chicken Francese.

Pierce took a bite of the perfectly cooked chicken. "Hon, you've outdone yourself," he said, his mouth full, "This is delicious."

She bowed her head slightly and raised her glass.

Between bites, they talked about the usual things people talk about at the dinner table—their children, weather, news, and finances.

Belly full, Pierce drank the last of his wine and said, "Let me help you clear the table. I'll fill you in on my conversation with Iggy when we're comfortably sitting in the living room."

"No room for a piece of coconut cream pie?" she asked.

"Oh wow. You made my favorite, but between that steak at lunch, and your scrumptious dinner, I'm about to explode," he said. "Maybe I'll have a piece with an espresso later … way later."

"All right, Howie," Louise said.

After they cleared the table and started the dishwasher, Pierce replenished their flutes, and they carried them into the living room where they sat comfortably next to each other on the sofa.

Pierce turned to Louise and nonchalantly said so as not to

alarm her, "Iggy called, asking me to look into Mr. Rudolph's death at Coral Bells."

"Don't tell me that's a homicide," Louise said, startled.

So much for trying to treat the call matter-of-factly.

"Not exactly. I visited Coral Bells today and spoke to a Mr. Miller."

"Oh, Mr. Miller," Louise said. "Nice man. He's been attending my cooking demonstrations since the beginning. Mr. Rudolph had attended a few classes before his death. They were best friends."

"Yes. I know."

"I gave Mr. Rudolph a couple of recipes for a dinner party he was planning." She shook her head. "It's all so sad. He worked hard and wanted to show everyone what he'd learned."

"Mr. Miller called the police the day after he found Mr. Rudolph's body, certain his friend did not die of natural causes," Pierce said.

Louise sat up. "He did?"

"Fraid so. From what he told me, a few things are worth investigating."

"If Mr. Miller has concerns, I'm sure you'll get to the bottom of it."

"Hope so… *there is* a person on my radar."

"Who?"

"The handyman."

"Mace? What makes him a suspect?"

"No, not a suspect," Pierce said, shaking his head, "but I am interested in knowing more about him. How well do you know him?"

"Not well at all. I've spoken with him a few times. He's pleasant enough but, I don't know …"

"What?" he said taking a sip of wine.

"He's always smiling. It's not natural."

Pierce almost choked, laughing. Louise pushed his shoulder, almost causing him to spill his drink.

"Oops, sorry," she said, "but don't laugh. I'm serious."

"Yes, dear," Pierce said, still laughing.

"I mean, how does a person go about his day smiling all the time? It's creepy. You don't suppose he's one of those people who are hurting and hide their true feelings behind a smile, only to commit suicide or, worse, go on a shooting spree?"

Pierce stopped laughing. "No, honey. That's not the impression I got at all."

"I hope not, because that would be tragic."

To lighten the mood, Pierce said, "Other than he smiles all the time, is there something else about the handy-dandy-handyman?"

Louise laughed at his description of Mace and asked, "Did you see all the keys dangling from his belt?" She sipped her wine.

Pierce did the same before he answered. "I did," he said.

"Once I overheard someone tell Mace he'd lost his apartment key. Mace told him he would unlock the door for him," Louise said.

Pierce suspected those keys dangling from Mace's chain are masters, possibly putting him inside Rudolph's apartment on the morning of his death.

"Makes sense. He carries around a lot of keys," said Pierce.

"I wouldn't feel comfortable if anyone, other than our girls, had keys to our house," Louise said, with a concerned look on her face.

Worrying Louise is why Pierce didn't like to discuss his cases with her. To put her at ease, he explained, "It's not unusual for managers of apartment buildings to have duplicate or master keys to all the units. Calling a locksmith every time someone gets locked out is not cost-effective, and in case of fire, there's no time to waste calling for a locksmith. For a place like Coral

Bells, where everyone is over the age of fifty, losing keys probably happens often."

"I suppose so."

"And remember, if a tenant has a medical emergency and calls for help, Mace will give first responders access if the tenant is unable to unlock his door. But from what I saw this afternoon, these people seem pretty healthy."

"Yes, of course," Louise said, "but I would think someone in the management office would entrust those keys to the security guards, not that I have any reason to suspect Mace of breaking into people's apartments."

"I'm sure they wouldn't have given the handyman those keys if he hadn't passed a background check," Pierce said, deciding to check Mace's background.

"I suppose so," Louise agreed, feeling less troubled.

Pierce wanted to get off the subject of Mace. "Have you ever witnessed any disagreements involving Mr. Rudolph and anyone else?"

"Not personally, no, but last week, I overheard Mr. Miller tell Mr. Rudolph not to pay attention to what Jamie said."

"Jamie? The bible studies guy?"

"Yes, Jamie Alinsky. Have you met him?"

"No, but someone told me about him. I heard he started the bible group a couple of years ago."

"I don't know about that, but I heard Mr. Rudolph had recently taken it over. Mr. Rudolph liked to disrupt the class with his arguments. Jamie had enough and walked out. Some members left the group shortly after Jamie did." Louise grabbed Pierce's arm and asked, "Howie, do you think someone killed Mr. Rudolph?"

He looked into her eyes and said, "No, it doesn't appear that way."

"If you say so. Makes me uneasy to think there might be a murderer lurking about at Coral Bells."

Pierce reached for her hand and gently squeezed it. "Chances are, if this is a homicide, and I'm not sure it is, the killer may have had something against Mr. Rudolph and is not hanging around waiting to get caught."

"Like someone who knew him before coming to live at the residence?" she asked.

"Exactly. In any case, don't you worry. I'll get to the bottom of this."

Louise remained pensive for a moment. "Howie, you don't suppose Mr. Alinsky held a grudge against Mr. Rudolph? After all, Mr. Rudolph took his class away from him."

Although Pierce was aware people kill for unbelievably absurd reasons than being pushed out of one's group, he asked, "Honey, do you honestly think Mr. Alinsky could have committed a murder?"

"No, not really," she said.

"Chances are Mr. Rudolph died of heart failure as the coroner said. Now finish your wine and don't think about this anymore. I promise you have nothing to fear." He leaned over and kissed her, sorry he had broken his own rule.

11

Pierce ran up the stairs, feeling like a homicide detective again. Despite his excitement, he didn't forget to run his fingers over the Bloodhound Investigations lettering before entering his outer office.

Not since closing his last homicide investigation had Howard Pierce felt like himself. Sure, his PI work gave him satisfaction, but he sorely missed unraveling murder investigations. Occasionally, when Sergeant Ramirez had asked for his help in doing background checks or surveilling suspects, he always felt let down when, after turning over his report, his involvement in the case ended. Iggy had dropped this case in his lap, and he was going to run with it until he solved it, one way or another.

Not wasting a moment, as soon as he entered the office, he announced, "Ruby, please clear my calendar for the rest of the day."

A flutter of curls swung around Ruby's head as she turned from her computer screen. "What gives?" she said. "Win the lottery or something?"

"In a manner of speaking." He pulled up the chair next to her desk and straddled it, facing the chair back.

"I'm going to investigate a homicide at the Coral Bells Adult Living apartments."

Ruby sat up. "A homicide?"

"Yes. Everyone has taken for granted the victim died of natural causes, but there are holes in that assumption. Won't be easy. At the moment, evidence is non-existent, but my gut says we have a homicide to investigate."

"Wow, how exciting. What do you need me to do?"

"I'm going to prepare a list of names for you to dig up anything you can on them. The people on your list are probably not responsible for Mr. Rudolph's death, but I need to eliminate them. I'll be working on gathering information for the ones I suspect may have been involved."

Ruby smiled. "Anything you need, boss."

"Thanks. You might have to work some overtime until we've solved this."

Ruby clicked her tongue. "I'd be happy to work on something other than these boring insurance cases we've been doing lately. A change of pace will break the monotony."

"Like I always say, you're a peach," said Pierce.

They both laughed.

"Do I have anything important going on today?"

"No, nothing that involves you going out in the field, but you still need to meet with Mrs. Lebron. She's anxious to see what you've turned up."

"All right. See if she can come in sometime this afternoon."

"Will do."

"Messages?"

"You have a message from a Mr. Frank Irizarry. Wants you to call him when you get a chance. Said there's no hurry." She tore the pink message slip from its pad and gave it to Pierce.

"Anything else?"

"You need to fax your report to the Quissk Insurance

Company. I left it on your desk." She glanced at her message pad, "and Mr. Miller phoned... *twice*. Need his number?"

"No. I got it. Thanks, Ruby."

"Here," she said, holding out the pink slip, "so you won't forget to call Mr. Miller."

"Okay, thanks."

Pierce got up and turned the chair around to its proper position. At the coffee machine, he poured a mug full and carefully carried the hot cup into his office. The Quissk report Ruby had typed from his notes sat in the middle of his desk. He placed the two message slips next to the phone, brought the coffee up to his lips, and gingerly took a sip before sitting. *First things first.*

He swiftly leafed through the insurance report, confident in Ruby's penchant for perfection, and signed the relevant page, already tagged with a yellow flag. After scanning the report into the insurance folder on his computer, he faxed the documents to the insurance company, along with the bill Ruby had prepared. He then put the documents into a folder and dropped it in the outbox for filing.

Pierce meant to return the phone calls, but sipping his coffee, his mind focused on the murder. With the last sip of coffee, he leaned back in his chair and closed his eyes. As was his custom when feeling out a crime, Pierce imagined the killer unlocking the door to Mr. Rudolph's apartment, dripping water from his wet clothing as he walked toward the bedroom, smudging the floor with every step. He checks on his intended victim, who is asleep, and kills him. Pierce theorized if Mr. Rudolph had been awake, the killer would have had to incapacitate him, perhaps using another method other than holding his CPAP mask so forcefully over Rudolph's face it caused a heart attack.

And why a hand towel? Was it to dry himself from the rain, or for another reason? Miller found the deceased wearing the

CPAP mask. If the killer took the trouble to pose Rudolph as if he were asleep, did he remove the mask after the kill to wipe Rudolph's face and then put it back on? The latex gloves found in the wastebasket of someone allergic to latex were most likely worn to conceal fingerprints, but since the death was not ruled suspicious, there was no need to dust for prints.

Pierce blew out his breath and sat up. *It's gonna be hard to pin this on someone.*

He grabbed the pink slips, choosing the message from the unknown caller first. *This might be a new client.*

After the third ring, Pierce was about to hang up, when a groggy-sounding voice answered, "This is Frank."

"Mr. Irizarry?"

"Yeah. Who's calling?"

"This is Howard Pierce, returning your call."

"Oh yes. Sorry if I sounded rude. You caught me dozing."

"How may I help you?" asked Pierce.

"I'm not calling because I need help. I'm calling to offer you my services."

Pierce rolled his eyes, thinking this was a telemarketer. "Thank you, but I'm not interested."

He was about to hang up when Irizarry said, "I recognized you when you visited Coral Bells yesterday."

Pierce put the phone on speaker. *Of course, Frank, the security guard. Shit.*

"You're the daytime security guard at Coral Bells," Pierce coolly said.

"Good memory."

"How did you find me?" Pierce asked, aware Irizarry had burned his cover.

"A couple of years ago, you solved a homicide case that hit the newspapers and the airwaves. At the press conference, I liked the way you stuck to the facts and gave your team credit for solving the case—very impressive. When I saw you at the residence, I figured you were there to investigate a murder."

Pierce had reluctantly held that press conference because of pressure from his superiors, who stressed politicians would be attending. That case had made headlines not only in Pennsylvania but in New York City. A big case like the one the detective squad solved was good publicity for the precinct, his captain had argued. Pierce had no choice but to attend.

Pierce frowned. "So you think someone has committed a murder at Coral Bells?"

"When I saw you, I figured you were there to investigate a homicide. The only person who has died recently is Mr. Rudolph. They said he died of a heart attack, but seeing you there got me thinking they got it wrong."

Another detective wannabe. Pierce had to shut this guy down.

"I'm not a homicide detective anymore, Mr. Irizarry."

"Really? I thought the private eye agency was part of your cover."

Does this guy know something of value, or is he the killer trying to find out if I suspect him?

"It's not a cover, Mr. Irizarry. I *am* a private investigator."

Frank sighed. "If you say so, Mr. Pierce, but then why were you at Coral Bells under an assumed name?"

Probably got my alias from Monica, thought Pierce. "I'm not at liberty to divulge what I was doing at Coral Bells."

"No, of course not. I get it. Anyway, I'll keep you informed if I hear or see anything suspicious. By the way, between you and me, that crazy bitch who tortured Mr. Romero on that last case of yours got what she deserved."

Geez!

"All right, but please keep your distance if you see me at Coral Bells again."

"Yes, sir. You can count on me."

Pierce imagined him saluting.

"And please, don't go around questioning anyone. That will make people nervous."

"Don't worry. I'll keep my eyes and ears open and will call you if I see or hear anything suspicious."

Pierce shook his head. "All right."

Frank stammered, "uh, it's my pleasure, uh, if you need anything, please, call me."

"Will do. Thanks again. Goodbye." Pierce ended the conversation before Frank asked to be deputized.

When he hung up, Pierce opened his notebook and read over the comments he had hastily jotted down in his car. Grabbing a legal pad, he wrote his impressions of the people who might be responsible for Mr. Rudolph's death. He divided the list in two, adding Frank Irizarry's name to his list of people of interest. He walked into the outer office carrying Ruby's half of the list.

"Here it is, Ruby. We have our work cut out for us."

Ruby grabbed the list. "I'll get started on this right away."

"You don't have to do it all today, though. I know it's a lot."

"Come on, boss. I can't wait to get involved in a murder investigation," she said. "Don't you worry about *me*."

Pierce thanked his lucky stars for sending him such an amiable and hard-working assistant and walked back into his office where he got to work, forgetting to return Mr. Miller's phone call.

By late afternoon, he'd run background checks and checked criminal databases, employment histories, and public records, for the people he thought worthy of scrutiny, taking a half-hour break to eat his lunch at his desk and later, to speak with Mrs. Lebron, who left his office in tears.

He stretched his arms wide and looked at the stacks of paper haphazardly arranged on his desk. All the information he could find online, which was substantial if you knew how to surf the web, was going to take some time to go through it all.

Can't do everything in one day.

Pierce got up and poked his head out his office door. "How are you doing, Ruby?"

"Good. Got half the list done," she said, without turning away from the computer screen.

"Excellent." He looked at his watch. "It's after six. Why don't you call it a day? You can pick it up tomorrow."

"I'll just finish with Mr. Jackson. Not much more to go. Already have most of his information."

"Fine, but don't stay too much longer."

"I won't."

He went back into his office and organized the piles into one. At the end of the day, Pierce felt satisfied with the preliminary data he'd collected.

Just as he logged off the computer, Ruby walked in. "I'm leaving now unless you want me to go over what I've found."

"We can do that tomorrow. You go on home, Ruby. Thanks for staying late."

She grabbed the contents of his outbox. "You're welcome."

"Have a good night, Ruby."

"You too. Don't forget to return those calls if you haven't already."

"Oh, yes. Got one more call to make. Thanks for the reminder."

Ruby waved goodbye and hastened out, her long curls swinging in harmony with her stride.

Pierce checked his pad where he had written Miller's number and dialed. Anticipating a lengthy conversation, he put the phone on speaker and leaned back in his chair.

"Hello."

"Mr. Miller. It's Howard Pierce. Sorry for getting back to you so late."

"I've been beside myself all day, waiting for your call."

Surprised by his annoyance, Pierce asked, "Have you got new information for me?"

"I'll say. I ran into Mrs. Garcia as I was heading to the laundromat this morning. She told me that on the morning of Wane's death she saw someone entering his apartment. That *proves* someone murdered Wane," he said, his voice shrill.

All ears, Pierce asked, "Who is Mrs. Garcia?"

"Mrs. Guadalupe Garcia, Wane's neighbor."

"Is it possible Mrs. Garcia saw you when you went to talk to Mr. Rudolph about the shopping list?"

"No," he said, his voice rising. "I didn't knock on Wane's door until seven-thirty. She said she saw someone enter Wane's apartment earlier."

"Calm down, Mr. Miller. Start at the beginning."

Miller took a deep breath. "Mrs. Garcia lives on the fourth floor, across from Wane's apartment."

Pierce got up to pace. "Was she going out or coming in when she saw someone at Mr. Rudolph's apartment?"

"Neither. She told me she wakes up at six in the morning every day like clockwork. On the morning of Wane's death, she was in her kitchen preparing a pot of tea, when she heard a noise out in the hallway. She looked through her door's peephole and saw a man standing in front of Wane's door."

"Did she recognize him?"

"She said she thought it was me waiting for Wane to answer the door."

"Did she see him enter or when he left the apartment?"

"I think when he entered, but she didn't bother to look after that."

"Thank you for the information. Again, I apologize for not getting back to you sooner."

"I know you're busy. Sorry for calling twice."

"No need for you to apologize. I'll go speak to Mrs. Garcia tomorrow. Try to relax."

"I'll try."

After his phone call, Pierce sat at his desk for a while, thinking about the significance of Mrs. Garcia's observation. Someone other than Miller was at Rudolph's apartment that morning, which added weight to Miller's suspicion of murder.

Tomorrow will be a busy day. Better get an early start.

12

Frank Irizarry did not come from a long line of police officers. No one in his family had ever worked in law enforcement in any capacity. His interest in solving crimes began as a teen when a child was abducted from his neighborhood. Worried his younger brother could be next, he volunteered to put up flyers, convinced his friends to form a neighborhood watch, and closely monitored the news. Police eventually found the boy unharmed. Frank breathed a sigh of relief when they caught the woman responsible for the kidnapping and arrested her, but he worried someone else might do the same.

Ever since then, wherever Frank lived, he followed every kidnapping and homicide reported on the local news. He filled notebooks with newspaper clippings, imagining himself the detective who cracked the case. After high school, Frank tried to join the police department, but they weren't hiring. He tried again the following year and failed the test. When he tried again, better prepared, he was told because of the merger, the Stroud Area Regional Police had a full roster—another disappointment.

Failure to land a police officer position, Frank worked as a night watchman in one warehouse or store after another. The security guard jobs had given him plenty of downtimes to indulge in his hobby—following crime stories and solving them in his imagination, but he thought if he were ever to learn detective work, he needed to be around people to study. When the job at Coral Bells opened up, he jumped at it. Working there allowed him to hone his observational skills.

It's no wonder when he saw Pierce at Coral Bells, Frank read it as a sign he would finally become involved in police work. It took all his willpower not to run over to Pierce and shake his hand. When the detective acknowledged his nod, Frank felt like an equal. It was the best day of his life.

And although he'd been reluctant to doubt Pierce's reason for snooping around the apartments under an assumed name, Frank found it hard to do so. *Wane Rudolph died, and a couple of days later, former Detective Howard Pierce shows up. Nah*, he thought. *This has to be a homicide investigation, and I'm gonna help him solve the case.*

Frank looked at the time. Two hours left until his shift ended and guests were still in the building. It seemed to him the beautiful summer evening had been busier than usual. Normally, Monica dealt with the bulk of visitors and telephone calls during the day, but for some reason, more residents than usual had people over. Between answering calls, directing guests to the restaurant or apartments, and answering inquiries, Frank could not begin his investigative work. It quieted down by eight, but Frank thought he better not leave his post until all visitors had gone home. By nine o'clock, the last of the guests had departed the premises, and the residents were in their apartments. "Finally," he muttered. "What a day."

After checking the locks at the unisex salon and the fitness center, Frank stopped in at the restaurant to see if he could get a snack before they locked up for the night. Men were busy vacuuming and stacking chairs as he maneuvered his way toward the kitchen, careful not to trip over the vacuum hose or bump into the crew.

"Hey there, Tony," called Frank, sauntering into the kitchen.

Tony turned away from the walk-in freezer. "Hey, Frank. Looking for a snack?" he grinned knowingly.

"You know it," Frank said.

"I gotcha. Saved a couple of macarons for ya. Let me get 'em."

"Thanks, Tony."

Reaching for a napkin-covered plate from the overhead cupboard, Tony said, "Lucky I was able to hide these. We ran out of almost everything tonight." He offered the plate to Frank. "Here you go. Grab yourself a cup of coffee, if there's any left in that urn, before I clean it out."

"Thanks," Frank said. He reached for the plate and walked over to the coffee station. The spout poured about two-thirds of a cup before sputtering the last of the coffee into his cup. "Just made it," said Frank to no one. Tony had gone into the walk-in.

Frank leaned against the counter, munching on the cookies, drinking his coffee, and watching Tony when he came back to clean the urn.

When it looked like Tony had finished, Frank thought he'd start his investigation. "Let me ask you a question," he said.

"What's up?" said Tony, coming over to Frank.

"You know about the death of one of our residents, right?"

"Sure. People can't shut up about it."

"Notice anything suspicious that morning or a few days prior?"

"Suspicious? Like what? Heard that guy died of a heart attack."

"Sure," Frank shrugged his shoulders, "but you know me. Can't help playing a cop."

Tony laughed. "Yeah."

"So, think back. Notice anything out of the ordinary happen around that day?"

Tony thought for a moment and said, "Can't think of anything."

"Just thought you might've heard something," Frank said.

"No, sorry, Frank."

"Hey, no problem. I'm just being curious."

Frank popped the last bit of cookie into his mouth and slurped the few drops of coffee left in his cup. He put the cup and dish on the counter. "Thanks again for the snack," he said.

"Any time, pal," said Tony.

"Better get on with my rounds then. Leaving soon?" he asked.

"Almost done."

"Okay then. See you up front."

"Yeah," said Tony, picking up Frank's used dishes.

When Frank walked into the dining room, the cleaning crew whispered amongst themselves as they walked out into the lobby. Frank followed them to the front desk and took the timesheet out of the drawer. He watched until everyone had signed out. "Goodnight fellas," he said, initialing their entries.

"Goodnight," they chorused.

Frank was just about to close the door when he spotted Tony rushing toward him.

"Don't shut the door, Frank. I'm outta here too." He grabbed the sheet and hastily signed out.

Frank held the door open. "Anyone else left in the restaurant?"

"Nope," said Tony. "Everyone's gone home." He smirked, "I'm the last one, as usual."

"Have a good night, Tony."

"You too."

Frank went back to the desk to finish checking the timesheet. All employees had left the building except for him.

It was now nine forty-five—too early to bolt the front door. Although he doubted anyone was going to come in before ten, Frank waited. To pass the time, he sat at the receptionist's desk and opened a card game on the computer, but he couldn't concentrate thinking of possible suspects. Frank homed in on one person he believed could have pulled off a murder. He ripped off a piece of paper from the memo pad and grabbed a pen, stowing the items in his pocket.

Ten o'clock and no one had come in since the restaurant crew left. Frank turned off the computer, locked the front door, and tried all the doors on the first level to make sure no one had inadvertently forgotten to lock up. He rode the elevator to the top floor. After checking the management office door, he walked down the stairs, stopping at every floor. Frank had a strong work ethic and completed his rounds when all he wanted to do was continue his investigation. Making sure everything was quiet on all the floors, he then proceeded to the lower level.

In front of Mace Leyton's caged workroom, he peered inside for a few minutes, eagerly searching for something—anything to tie Mace to the murder. He could see nothing of interest in that crowded room, but determined to get inside, reached for the padlock and ran his finger over the code etched beneath the brand name. He pulled out the memo paper and pen from his pocket. With the paper flattened in his left hand and pen in his right, he copied the code. Deep in thought, Frank took the stairs slowly to the main lobby.

The next morning, Frank visited a locksmith. It didn't take the owner long to make a duplicate key after verifying Frank's identity and confirming his employment. While waiting, Frank tapped his foot, anxious to get the key that would get him inside that room.

That evening, fidgeting in his chair and checking the time every few minutes, Frank wondered if Mace would stay a few hours past his quitting time, as he so often did, sometimes staying as late as midnight. He breathed a sigh of relief when Mace finally walked by at twenty after seven and scratched his name on the sheet. "Night," he said, and dashed out the door. Frank said, "Goodnight, Mace," but he had already left.

Frank pushed the reception chair back and strolled around the lobby, full of nervous energy. Residents were still milling about or going out for a stroll. It took all of Frank's resolve not to shoo them back into their apartments. He heard the reception phone ring and ran to answer it, staying put for the time being.

By eight-thirty, Frank's leg had been nervously bouncing underneath the table, waiting for his chance to get into Mace's workroom. Once again, he walked around the lobby, checking doors. The restaurant had not yet closed. He took a peek through the glass and saw the crew cleaning up. Most residents had settled down for the night, but he could not lock the front door yet. He found two people commenting on the hot weather in the sitting room as they watched the meteorologist on TV. They both looked up when they noticed Frank standing at the entrance. "Hi, Frank," they greeted.

"Good evening, gentlemen."

They stared at him, expecting Frank to say something.

Not sure what to say, Frank muttered, "Don't stay up too late," sounding foolish for implying they should go to bed. He turned and quickly walked away.

"We won't," he heard one of them say.

After patrolling the floors, Frank checked on the people watching TV. All quiet, he looked inside the restaurant. The lights were off, and the door locked. He then returned to reception and opened the front door, looking for stragglers. He made sure everyone had signed the sheet he had carelessly left on the desk after Mace signed it, and initialed the entries before locking the sheet in the drawer. Checking his watch, it read nine-fifteen, forty-five minutes to go. Frank wanted to lock up for the night, but resisted the urge. It wouldn't do for someone to come in late, bang on the door, and make a complaint about why they found the door bolted before ten. He had no choice but to wait.

Every few minutes, Frank checked his watch listening to music on his Walkman, but he barely paid attention to the music. By ten o'clock, no one had come in or out after Mace left for the evening. *I Shoulda shut the door earlier,* he thought, turning the lock.

Hustling down the stairs, Frank retrieved the new key from his pants pocket. Taking a deep breath to calm his nerves, he tried the key. At first, it felt tight in the lock, but it clicked open after jiggling it a few times. The metal door creaked when Frank pushed it. Instinctively, he froze, and shook his head when he realized he was alone. *Some handyman,* Frank thought. *Can't even oil his door hinges.*

Frank had never been inside Mace's workroom before, it being locked when he made his nightly rounds. Not sure where to begin, he scratched his head and looked around. Tools were either hanging on the hooks on a pegboard or spread on a long table, presumably where Mace did his repairs. A workman's horse with a two-by-four propped on top had a hand saw on it, ready for cutting. Next to a tall metal garbage bin stuffed to the brim, a straw broom and dustpan filled with sawdust leaned against it. Frank stared, disgusted at the piles of newspapers on the cement floor and grimaced at a soot-covered fan bolted to the wall.

He peeked at his wristwatch. *Ten-ten. Plenty of time.*

It seemed Mace had been repairing a window fan on the worktable. Mace had unscrewed the fan blades from the motor and placed them carelessly on the crowded table, the oil can, and Phillip's screwdriver nearby. Frank almost touched one of the dusty blades but remembered not to disturb anything, especially dust-covered. He took a pair of rubber gloves from his pocket to inspect a heavy metal toolbox next to the fan blades. It would not do for him to leave DNA behind to confuse the forensics team Frank was sure would be swarming all over the work-space once he found the evidence needed to accuse Mace of Mr. Rudolph's murder. Nervously trying to fit the gloves on his sweaty fingers, he cursed in frustration, *fucking shit! Relax*, he told himself, blowing into the gloves and easily pulling them on.

Gloves on, the urge to wipe off the dust from the blades momentarily took his mind off his mission. He shook his head and focused on a heavy metal toolbox next to the blades. Snap-ping the latches, he opened the box and whistled. *Jeez, this guy has more tools than a hardware store.*

Believing killers often took souvenirs after they killed, Frank walked around, examining everything, hoping to find incrimi-nating evidence linking Mace to Mr. Rudolph's murder. A crate full of videos sat on the floor gathering dust. Frank's imagina-tion got the better of him, thinking the videos were of Mace's murder victims. He bent and inspected them, disappointed they were all how-to videos. *So this is how he gets by.*

He looked around for the VCR and spotted it jammed into a cardboard box next to other cardboard boxes underneath what looked like an old poker table. About to give up, he noticed a small refrigerator sitting on top of a metal two-drawer file cabi-net, which didn't look sturdy enough to hold it. Its sides over-lapped the cabinet. Inside were two bottles of water, a can of soda, one beer can, and a six-pack. *Does he drink on the job? Shit.*

Frank gently closed the refrigerator door, fearing a slam would knock the whole thing over. He bent and held one hand on the refrigerator, and with the other, opened the file cabinet. The first drawer contained napkins, plastic spoons, a bottle opener, straws, and an old deck of cards. About to open the second drawer, out of the corner of his eye, he saw a crumbled piece of paper on the floor. He bent to pick it up. His eyebrows shot up when he read, 'See you tonight. Looking forward to our weekly card game. Will bring beer,' signed by G.

Frank put the note in his pocket, certain it was important,

and opened the bottom drawer, where a metal box took up all the space. He picked it up and walked over to the table, where he unlatched the case. "Huh?"

He picked up one of the many bits inside the compartments, put it back, then selected another. He didn't know what he'd found, but felt he'd hit the jackpot. Lifting the tray, he found a diagram. Frank spent the next few minutes comparing it to the various parts.

The more he identified the assortment of pins, including deadbolt and pin springs, plug clips, cylinder caps, spanner tool, gauge pin tweezers, and other tools, including brass key blanks, a pippin file, pickle fork, and code cutter, the more excited he became. *Locksmith tools.*

Grinning ear to ear, Frank let his imagination run wild, placing Mace in Mr. Rudolph's apartment on the morning of his death. His eyes darted over the instructions for making keys, while his heart beat with excitement, imagining Mace bent over his worktable, making a key to Mr. Rudolph's apartment.

Wait a minute.

His smile collapsed, and he slapped his forehead with the palm of his hand. *Fuck me. Mace has master keys. He has no reason to make keys. What an idiot I am.*

Crestfallen, he closed the case and returned it to the cabinet drawer. Head bowed and feeling like a failure, Frank let himself out, remembering to lock the door.

13

Pierce was just about to take a bite out of his wife's freshly baked banana bread when he remembered he hadn't asked Mr. Miller for an introduction to Mrs. Garcia. It wouldn't do for him to show up at her door asking questions.

After breakfast, he headed to the den and picked up the telephone. Mr. Miller readily agreed to introduce him to his neighbor. Pierce sensed Miller's involvement in the investigation had lifted his spirits, although an introduction is all Pierce needed from him at the moment.

Louise was wiping down the kitchen counter when Pierce grabbed her by the waist. Leaning in for a kiss, he said, "If you happen to see me at Coral Bells, please don't say hi, as much as you may want to." He squeezed her a little tighter.

"It will be hard to ignore your animal magnetism, but I'll do my best," she said, and winked.

He winked back, and they both smiled. "What delectable dish are you teaching the class today?" Pierce asked.

"It's a variation of an old recipe for stroganoff. I hope it goes over well."

"I'm sure it will. Everything you cook is delicious."

"Go on now," said Louise, pushing him affectionately with her hip.

Pierce kissed her again. "Have a wonderful day, hon."

"You too."

———

MONICA HUNG up on a call in time to see Pierce walking toward her. "Hello. I'll ring Mr. Miller for you."

"Hi, Monica. Thanks."

Pierce did not wait for Monica to complete her call to Miller. Instead, he signed the log, waved to her, and headed toward the elevator.

Although clean-shaven and impeccably dressed in a crisp buttoned-down cotton shirt and linen trousers, Jenaro Miller looked like he hadn't slept in days. Pierce hated to disturb him.

"Thank you for coming. I can take you to see Mrs. Garcia now," Miller anxiously said, stepping out of his apartment, key in hand.

He must've been standing by the door waiting for me.

Pierce understood Miller's desire to be present when he interviewed Mrs. Garcia, but he didn't want him to influence anything the neighbor had to say. Pierce thought he'd better make himself clear.

"Before we head down, can we take a moment to talk?"

"I telephoned Guadalupe earlier. She's expecting us," Miller protested.

"This will only take a minute," said Pierce.

Miller looked confused. He'd already conveyed the conversation he had with Mrs. Garcia to Pierce, and didn't understand what else there was to talk about. Still, he opened the door wider and led Howard into the kitchen, where they sat at the kitchen counter.

"Mr. Miller," Pierce said, facing him, "it's my habit to interview potential witnesses alone. Sometimes people get influenced, perhaps subconsciously, by anyone else present. You understand?"

"You don't have to worry about me. I won't say a word."

"Just by your presence alone, she might withhold something she doesn't want to say in front of you."

Miller's shoulders sagged. "All right. I'll make the introductions and take my leave."

"It would be best. People speak freely when someone they know isn't part of the interview."

Miller pushed back his stool. "Shall we go now?" he said, disappointed.

"Yes, please. Lead the way."

Mrs. Guadalupe Garcia, a short, middle-aged, small-framed woman with jet-black hair, tied in a neat bun, and wearing an apron, answered the door. The scent of baked peaches filled the air.

"Good morning, Guadalupe," Miller said.

"*Hola*, Jenaro."

"This is Mr. Howard Martal," he said.

She smiled at Pierce. "Nice to meet you, Mr. Martal." Her dimpled smile softened her face, making her appear years younger.

"I'll leave you two to talk," said Miller, ready to take his leave.

"Oh, aren't you coming in? *I have a slice of peach pie with your name on it,*" she teased in a singsong voice.

Miller shot a quick look at Pierce and gave her a sad smile. "I'll be back after your meeting. Thanks," he said and dashed away.

For a fleeting moment, Mrs. Garcia looked baffled by Miller's quick getaway. She turned to Pierce. "Mr. Martal, please come in. We can talk in the kitchen," she said, where she grabbed the percolator off the stove and began filling two mugs before she asked, "Coffee?"

Pierce didn't want any, having had his usual fill at breakfast, but since she had already poured it, he said, "Yes, thank you."

"Cream and sugar?"

"Black, please."

Pierce looked around. On the kitchen counter, a rolling pin dusted with flour sat on a wooden board, also floured. A bag of sugar, flour, various spices, and a basket of fruit littered the counter. The pie cooling on a grill filled the room with the aromatic scent Pierce had inhaled as soon as she opened her front door.

"Please excuse the mess," she said. "As you can see, I've been baking."

"It smells wonderful in here."

"Thank you. Please sit."

Pierce pulled out a chair.

She carried the cups to the small table and set them down.

"Do you like peach pie?" she asked, turning away.

She's stalling. Nervous?

"I like any kind of pie," he said with a smile.

She pointed. "That's the peach pie I baked earlier." She took the pie off the grill and grabbed a knife. "I'll slice a piece for you."

Before he could reply, she cut into it.

"Still warm," she said, lifting the piece with a pie spade and filling a plate with a generous piece. She grabbed a fork out of the drawer and a napkin from the holder and put them in front of Pierce. "Enjoy," Mrs. Garcia said, taking a seat across from him.

"Thank you." Pierce took a bite. "This is good, Mrs. Garcia," he said with a mouth full.

"Glad you like it."

He was about to begin the interview when the oven timer rang.

"Excuse me." Mrs. Garcia picked up her untouched coffee cup and put it in the sink.

Definitely nervous.

Between bites of pie and sips of coffee, Pierce watched her grab a mitt hanging on the hook next to the oven and open the door. When she pulled out the oven grill, she turned and grabbed a toothpick out of its holder with her ungloved hand to test the doneness of the pie. Inspecting the dry toothpick, she inhaled deeply and said, "Perfect." She put on the other oven mitt and took it out, placing it on the trivet. With no more pies to fuss over, she sat across from Pierce, looking as if she'd rather be somewhere else.

"I'm sorry to interrupt your baking," Pierce said, drinking the last of his coffee.

"It's okay. Jenaro thinks I can help you prove that Mr. Rudolph didn't die of natural causes." She shook her head. "I can't believe someone murdered him in his apartment." She began twisting the folds of her apron and said, "That could have been me."

"It's not clear he was murdered, Mrs. Garcia. The medical examiner pronounced Mr. Rudolph died of a heart attack. Mr. Miller is not convinced, so I promised to do what I can to investigate the matter."

"Yes, but Jenaro told me the man I saw going into Wane's apartment was not him. Who else could it have been other than someone wishing to do harm?" she said, continuing to twist the folds of her apron.

"Don't you worry, ma'am. That's what I'm hoping to find out."

Pierce pulled his pad and pen out of his shirt pocket and flipped to a new page. Mrs. Garcia watched him carefully.

"How did you happen to see someone at your neighbor's apartment?"

"I was in the kitchen about to fill the teapot when I heard a very loud sneeze out in the hallway. I glanced at the clock and hurried to look through the peephole, concerned because it was so early. Maybe someone needed help I thought." She lowered her voice. "That's when I saw him."

"What time was that?"

"Sixteen minutes after six."

Pierce made a notation on his pad. 'Garcia saw a stranger at 6:16 a.m. Josephine was still on duty.'

"Did you see him knock?"

"No."

"Did you happen to notice if his hand was holding the doorknob?"

She scrunched her eyebrows. "What do you mean?"

"If Mr. Rudolph had answered the door, the man would have entered without touching the doorknob. If the stranger let himself in with a key, or if he picked the lock, then his hand would have been on the doorknob to push the door open. You see?"

"Yes. That makes sense, but, honestly, I didn't notice."

"That's okay. Go on," Pierce said.

"There's nothing more to tell. I only saw him for a second. I thought it was Jenaro."

"What made you think it was a man you saw?"

"What? Of course, it was a man. He was tall and had broad shoulders. Besides, I've never heard a woman sneeze that loud."

Pierce started firing off one question after another, concentrating on her reactions. In his experience, this line of questioning sometimes helped people remember details they thought they hadn't noticed.

"Did he have on a hat?"

"No, no hat."

"Hair, no hair?"

"He had hair."

"What color?"

She touched her forehead. "His dark hair appeared to be slicked down like he was caught in the rain."

"Did he wear glasses?"

"Glasses?" She tapped her fingers on the countertop and bit her lip, trying to remember. "I only saw him from the side for a second when he turned his head from side to side before going in, but no, I did not notice any glasses."

"What was he wearing?"

"I think it was a black raincoat."

She was now fidgeting in her seat, chewing on her bottom lip.

"You're doing fine, Mrs. Garcia," Pierce said.

"I can't believe I thought it was Jenaro I saw. He's not as big as that stranger. Oh my God. I shouldn't have jumped to conclusions."

"That's perfectly normal, Mrs. Garcia. You were expecting to see Mr. Miller. In that brief moment, looking through your peephole, you naturally assumed it was him. Even if you hadn't recognized the man in front of Mr. Rudolph's apartment, he may have been expected. You couldn't have known if that man meant Mr. Rudolph harm, and remember, we don't know if Mr. Rudolph opened the door for him."

She took in a breath, blew it out, and relaxed. "I suppose you're right."

"One last question. Did you happen to notice if he wore galoshes or rain boots?"

She shook her head. "No. Sorry."

"Not at all, Mrs. Garcia. You've been extremely helpful. I appreciate it very much."

He scribbled a few notes and closed his pad. "Thank you for the wonderful coffee and pie. You're a gifted baker."

She flashed her beautiful, dimpled smile. "Thank you."

"It was a pleasure meeting you," Pierce said.

"You as well."

At the door, Pierce said, "Please keep our conversation confidential. I don't want anyone speculating on Mr. Rudolph's death."

"Of course. I understand."

"Thank you for seeing me."

"You're welcome," she said and gently closed the door.

———

WHEN THE DOORS opened on the third floor, Chef Delacroix stood tall in the middle of the small elevator, taking up a good amount of space with his imposing figure. He smiled, stepping aside to let Pierce enter. "Hello. Mr. Martal, is it?"

"Yes," Pierce answered, glancing at the panel to make sure the lobby button was lit. "Nice to see you again, Chef."

"Still mulling over the decision to buy in here?"

"I'll probably have to wait a while. There aren't any single units available."

The chef smiled. "Well, you can't find a better place to live. Worth the wait for an apartment, but make sure Miss Santiago has you on the waiting list."

The elevator arrived at the lobby before Pierce could respond. "After you," Chef Delacroix said, extending his hand toward the open door.

"Thanks. Good seeing you again," said Pierce, stepping off the elevator.

"Same here."

Delacroix stared after him with a quizzical expression on his face watching Pierce sign out and wave at Monica before exiting the building.

Usually, when people looked at apartments, the chef only

saw them at the complimentary meal for prospective buyers. If they decided to buy, the next time he saw them was on moving day. Walking toward the restaurant, the chef thought, *If there is no apartment available at the moment, why is he here? Perhaps he knows someone who lives here, or…*

Sous Chef Janet had been on the lookout for her boss. As soon as he entered the kitchen, she announced, "sorrel is eighty-sixed."

All thoughts of the mysterious Martal vanished. Delacroix bellowed, "What the fuck happened?"

Used to the chef's outbursts, no one flinched except the young woman at the salad station, who almost dropped the salt she sprinkled on the lettuce. Most did their best not to become the target of the chef's tirades, keeping their heads down and tending to their tasks.

Unfazed, Janet answered, "They sent the delivery to the wrong restaurant."

"Incompetent sons of bitches," he said through clenched teeth.

"We should get a redelivery order in a couple of hours," explained Janet.

Delacroix sarcastically said, "Well, that's not gonna cut it, is it, Janet? Do we at least have the crab?"

"Yes, Chef."

"Then we'll make the soufflé, sans the sorrel, just fucking crab."

"Yes, Chef."

Delacroix walked over to the board and angrily scratched out the word *sorrel* from the soufflé appetizer.

Drama over, he walked around checking and tasting, making sure everything was to his satisfaction. That done, he opened the refrigerator, took out the lamb chops, and started preparing them for the main course.

———

BACK IN HIS OFFICE, Pierce looked over the notes of his conversation with Mrs. Garcia. He noted Josephine Devin, the security guard, was on duty at the time Mrs. Garcia said she heard someone sneeze out in the hallway. If the killer lived at Coral Bells, he would've had to be out in the rain before getting into Rudolph's apartment. If that's the case, what was he doing out so early in the morning, or perhaps he came home after an all-nighter? It makes more sense the killer did not live there but is an employee. In either case, the security guard would not have let him in if she didn't know him.

Pierce couldn't think of a plausible reason to approach Josephine Devin with questions. It would not do for him to track her down on her off hours. Showing up at midnight when she began her shift was out of the question, the same when she left work at eight in the morning. A friendly conversation with someone she knows would most likely get him the information he desired. Frank Irizarry came to mind. Pierce might not have a choice but to trust Irizarry, the only person aside from Miller who knows his real identity, but he put off deciding on Frank until he reviewed his background.

14

*P*ierce's head dropped onto his chest and bounced up like a rubber band. He opened his eyes and stretched his arms letting out a gaping yawn. "Oh shit," he said, glancing at his watch.

After his meeting with Mrs. Garcia, he had Ruby create files for his people of interest, labeling them by name. Not only did she do that, but she set up tabs within the folders titled Known Addresses, Employment History, Criminal Record, Background Check, Education, and Miscellaneous. She did the same for the ones on her list.

They both diligently worked on their lists, taking a dinner break when Ruby asked if she could order dinner. Pierce readily agreed sorry he hadn't thought about dinner himself. He sent Ruby home four hours past her quitting time, thanking her for her help and complimenting her for doing a great job.

"Didn't mean to keep you so late two nights in a row," Pierce said.

"That's all right, boss. I didn't notice the time either. It's all good."

"I appreciate that, Ruby. Go home now and get some rest."

"Okay. Goodnight, boss."

"Night, Ruby, and thanks again."

At midnight, Pierce turned off the lights and drove home.

The next day, he opened his eyes two hours past his usual time. He'd forgotten to set the alarm when he fell into bed.

Pierce called Ruby first thing.

"Bloodhound Investigations," answered Ruby's cheerful voice.

"Ruby. It's Howard."

"Morning, boss."

"Good morning. I don't think I have anything pending for this morning, do I?"

"Nothing that needs your immediate attention."

"Okay. I'll be in before lunch. Thank you again for working late last night."

"You're welcome."

"What smells so good?" he asked when he walked into the kitchen.

"Just finished testing a new recipe for the next cooking lesson," Louise said.

"Smells wonderful."

Without turning from the soapy dishes in the sink, Louise said, "I have to stop at the market for a few things before meeting the girls for lunch. Grab some coffee and make yourself some eggs or something. I'm running late."

"Okay." He reached for his wife.

"Howie, I have my hands in dishwater," she protested good-naturedly.

"I don't mind," he said. Pierce turned her around, and gave her a tight hug and a kiss, as water dripped from her gloves onto the floor.

"Thanks for letting me sleep in. I needed it."

"I figured."

"Have a great day, honey," he said, releasing her. "Give the girls my love," he said.

Louise smiled, shaking her head. "Have a good day yourself," she said, as she took off her gloves and pulled a handful of paper towels from the holder to wipe the floor.

Pierce did thirty minutes on the bike, showered, and dressed. After a quick breakfast of toast with jam and coffee, he felt invigorated.

In his office, Pierce glanced at the folders stacked on his desk but decided not to delve into them just yet. He wanted to find out more about the Rudolphs' son. Perhaps Ethan's death might give him another piece of the puzzle. Mr. Miller said the boy died during his junior high school years. Remembering how long his parents were married, Pierce took the calculator out of his desk drawer and punched in 2005, the year Lilly Rudolph died. He then deducted fifty-two years, the time the Rudolphs were married. That brought him to 1953. Because the Rudolphs were Catholic, Pierce assumed Ethan was born between 1954 and 1955. Adding twelve years when Ethan would have been starting junior high school brought him to 1966. He now had a rough timeline of the brief life of Ethan Rudolph.

Because he couldn't contact the New York City Department of Health for copies of birth and death certificates in an official capacity, Pierce spent the next two hours searching for newspaper obituaries for the years 1966 through 1968, keeping in mind the typical ages of middle school children.

Not finding anything on Ethan Rudolph's death, Pierce's frustration grew, despite the fact he knew it was not going to be easy finding information decades old. He leaned back in his chair and closed his eyes. *Where else might I find news of the boy's death besides a newspaper?*

Pierce sat up and grabbed the mouse, searching churches in the immediate neighborhood where the Rudolphs lived, concentrating on the period he had designated. He zeroed in on St.

Anthony's, the closest church to the vicinity where the Rudolphs lived, and the oldest one in the Bronx. He found the telephone number and dialed.

A woman's voice answered. "St. Anthony's."

"Hello. I was wondering if you keep records of births and deaths for your congregants."

"Yes, we do. Not only birth and death records but marriages and baptisms too. Are you looking for a specific record?"

"I'm interested in finding information about a death that occurred sometime around 1965 through 1968."

"Oh my," she said. "You'll have to speak to Father Carlway. He may be able to help you."

"Can you connect me to him, please?"

"He's not in at the moment, but if you leave your name and number, I'll have him return your call."

"My name is Howard Pierce. I'm a private investigator and owner of Bloodhound Investigations in East Stroudsburg, Pennsylvania."

"Private investigator?"

"Yes, Ma'am."

"Is it an urgent matter?"

"No, not urgent, but if Father Carlway could get back to me today, I would appreciate it."

"All right."

Pierce recited both his office and cell numbers. "He can reach me on my cell if I'm not in the office."

"I'll give him the message, Mr. Pierce."

"Thank you."

By late afternoon, Pierce's stomach began to growl. He wanted to do a new search for schools in Rudolph's neighborhood but needed to take a break. The morning's energy had worn off, and his tired eyes were blinking in and out of focus. He rubbed them and pushed back his chair.

When he opened the refrigerator, he noticed Ruby had

refilled it, taking care not to crush his lunch. He smiled and took out the hefty sandwich of leftover roast beef on wheat bread, with lettuce, tomato, and mustard he had brought from home. He pulled a mug out of the cupboard and filled his cup.

"Thanks for filling the fridge, Ruby," he said, carrying his sandwich and coffee.

"I bought peaches this time 'cause, you know," she smirked.

It took Pierce a second before he said, "You're a peach."

They both laughed, enjoying their usual joke.

Eating his sandwich, Pierce thought of the paperwork he had set aside for two likely people whose background checks revealed both had lived in or around Rudolph's home address at some point during the years the Rudolphs lived in the Bronx. Pierce hoped linking one or both of these people of interest to Wane or Lilly Rudolph, and perhaps their son would lead him to a motive.

Pierce laced his fingers and stretched out his arms, sitting comfortably in his office chair. *Here we go.*

He searched for junior high school yearbooks for the sixties and seventies but could find none. *Were there even yearbooks for middle schools in those days?*

The ringing telephone pulled him out of his contemplation.

"Howard Pierce."

"Mr. Pierce. This is Father Carlway returning your call."

"Yes. Thank you for getting back to me."

"I understand you're looking for information on a death that occurred over four decades ago?" Father Carlway asked in disbelief.

"Yes, Father. Do you keep records that old?"

"We do, but I'm curious. The secretary said you're a private investigator. May I ask what your interest is in finding the information you seek?"

"Not at all. A boy living in your neighborhood committed suicide around that time. At present, his father may have been the victim of a homicide. I'm trying to piece together a motive."

"And you think the two events are connected?" he asked.

"Maybe."

"Seems farfetched, if you don't mind my saying so."

Pierce had to agree, but he could not ignore the possibility the past might lead him to the killer. "There are two people presently living in my neck of the woods who lived in the Melrose neighborhood during the time the boy and his parents lived there. Although it's a long shot, I cannot ignore the coincidence."

There was a pause. Pierce waited.

Father Carlway said, "Are you assisting the police in this matter? Private Investigators don't usually get involved in homicide cases, do they?"

"No, not usually. I retired as a homicide detective. Because of my expertise and because there is scant evidence in this case, the police asked me to look into a claim from the decedent's friend that a homicide had been committed."

"I see. What are the names you are interested in?"

"Wane and Lily Rudolph, and their son, Ethan, who was perhaps twelve or a little older at the time of his death."

Father Carlway remained quiet for a moment. Pierce imagined the priest writing down the names.

"I'll have to consult my superior before undertaking a search of the archives. I'll get back to you. May I call you at this number?"

"Yes."

"All right."

"Thank you for your help, Father. I appreciate it."

"Goodbye, Mr. Pierce."

"Goodbye, Father."

Pierce hung up and reached for the pile that most interested him.

15

*F*ather Carlway was deep in thought. He'd just hung up with the private investigator and could think of no good reason why someone would be interested in a family whose son had died decades ago. If the child's father had indeed died under suspicious circumstances, how are the two deaths, decades apart, connected? he wondered.

Before bringing the matter up to his monsignor, he thought it best to do a little research on the private investigator. He reached for the computer mouse and typed in 'Bloodhound Investigations.' When he clicked on the website's link, it opened to Howard Pierce's smiling face, the caption, Bloodhound Investigations, above his photo.

In the bio section, mention of a few of Detective Howard Pierce's homicide investigations interested the priest; the Romero homicide, in particular. Wanting to know more, he found more articles in the local Pocono Record newspaper, including a picture of the news conference with the mayor standing next to an uncomfortable-looking detective. Satisfied with Howard Pierce's credentials, Father Carlway went straight to the monsignor. Pierce's distinctive career had convinced him a respected law enforcement officer had to have a good reason for needing the Church's help.

"Come in," Monsignor Sullivan said when he heard the knock on his door.

Father Carlway bowed his head and clasped his hands together. "Monsignor."

Monsignor Sullivan sat bent over his desk, writing a letter on the official church stationery. Peering over his wire-rimmed bifocals, he motioned for Father Carlway to take a seat. "Sit, sit. I'll be with you in a moment."

"Please, take your time."

Father Carlway looked around the room he'd admired ever since being assigned to St. Anthony's twenty years ago. While there had been some modern renovations to the church over the years, this office remained untouched. Original wood covered the walls displaying an antique cross between the portrait of the archbishop of New York, Cardinal Edward Egan, and the portrait of Pope Benedict XVI. The monsignor's oversized mahogany desk stood the test of time, with barely a scratch on it.

The priest tried not to focus on his superior's arthritic hand as he slowly moved the pen over the official church stationery. Although he appeared fragile, Father Carlway was keenly aware of Monsignor Sullivan's sharp intellect. Once he explained the reason for his visit, he hoped he could convince the monsignor to give him the blessing for the archival search.

A few minutes passed, but Monsignor Sullivan kept scribbling. *He must have just started the letter when I entered*, thought Father Carlway. He felt like an intruder and wanted to excuse himself, but didn't know how. After an interminable amount of time, the monsignor put down his pen and looked at the priest, who tried not to look bothered at the long wait.

"Sorry to keep you waiting, Father. How may I help you?"

Father Carlway cleared his throat. "I had a rather unusual

call today from a private investigator who used to be a homicide detective in Pennsylvania." He paused.

Monsignor Sullivan liked to listen without interruption when someone came to him with a problem or concern. He learned long ago he could not opine or give advice until the speaker had finished all he had to say. He said, "Go on."

The priest relayed everything Pierce had told him, ending with his request to go through the archives for information about the Rudolphs, based on the research he had done on Pierce.

The cleric scrunched his bushy, snow-white eyebrows. "I seem to remember a family with the surname Rudolph." He tapped his fingers on his desk and his eyes took on a blank stare. Suddenly, he slammed the desk with his hand, making Father Carlway jump.

"Yes. Wane and his wife, Lillian." He turned toward Father Carlway. "I was a young priest then, teaching the Catechism. Their son, Ethan, attended my class for a short while, although I could tell he'd rather have been somewhere else." He smiled at the memory.

Father Carlway asked, "Do you remember the circumstances of their son's death?"

The monsignor clicked his tongue and exhaled. "As I recall, Ethan overdosed on his mother's prescribed medication and a pint of his father's whiskey. Mrs. Rudolph was on Prozac for anxiety and depression. Was hospitalized once or twice for the affliction, but she assured me during one of our meetings that she had it under control." He shook his head. "Yes, she found him dead when she went to wake him for school. Can you imagine finding your child dead in his bed?" He tsk-tsked.

"No, I cannot." Father Sullivan answered.

"As I recall, the coroner said the boy died hours before his mother found him. Must have taken those pills as soon as he went to his room for the night."

"Before his death, had Mrs. Rudolph come to you for advice?"

"Occasionally she'd come by and ask for me. If not busy, I'd sit with her. I asked her to make an appointment to make sure I was available, but she never did. Just showed up when she was distressed. I advised her to bring her husband with her, but Mrs. Rudolph said he wouldn't come. Ethan's death plunged the poor woman back into a state of depression, more serious than she had previously suffered, as you can well imagine. She left her husband, but eventually returned to the marriage until her death."

Father Carlway bowed his head sympathetically.

"Blamed herself for not keeping the Prozac locked up. I did my best to convince her a troubled person would find a way to do what her son did. Of course, anything I said did not alleviate her guilt."

"Did Ethan leave a note?" Father Carlway asked, thinking that's what suicidal people did.

"Yes, more of a long letter than a note. Mrs. Rudolph confessed she hid it from the police and also from her husband, Wane."

"I can understand not wanting the police to see it, hoping the death be ruled an accident, but why hide the letter from her husband?" asked Father Carlway.

"She never said, at least not to me."

The monsignor's memory amazed Father Carlway.

"After the funeral, Mrs. Rudolph pleaded in the confessional that the letter be kept with her child's church records. She didn't want her son's last handwriting destroyed, no matter how painful the content. Said she couldn't bear to keep it but didn't have the heart to tear it up. I wanted to tell her I couldn't accept such a document, but I found it difficult to deny her."

Father Carlway tried to keep his disapproval out of his voice when he asked, "Isn't that unorthodox?"

"Yes, of course. I thought the letter belonged to the police, but the anguish in her voice silenced me and I accepted the letter. After her confession, I hid it in the archives as she requested."

"Did you read it, Monsignor?" Father Carlway dared to ask.

Monsignor Sullivan looked at the priest for a long moment, and finally answered, "I didn't think it appropriate, but yes, I read it."

Father Carlway swallowed, not wanting to pass judgment. He asked, "Do I have your permission to cooperate with the private investigator?"

"You do. If there is a connection between the death of the father and the son, from what you've told me, that PI is the perfect man to discover it."

Father Carlway rose. "Thank you for hearing me out, Monsignor."

"Let me know when you've located the records and bring them to me before you contact that investigator. I may want to meet with him. Perhaps he can explain how the past ties in with the present."

"Yes, Monsignor."

Father Carlway again bowed his respect and closed the door behind him. Now that he had a brief history of the Rudolphs, he was impatient to read Ethan's letter. Perhaps it would explain why the monsignor thought it best not to consult *his* monsignor before deciding to bury it away in the archives.

He wasted no time hurrying to the archive room.

16

*D*awn bathed the room in gentle sunlight filtering through the slats of the closed blinds. Pierce awoke from a restless night. He wanted to go back to sleep, but his mind was filled with questions about his current investigation. After a while, he got up, careful not to wake Louise. He pulled a shirt and pair of pants from the closet and underwear from his drawer, picked up his shoes, and carried the bundle into the bathroom. He showered and shaved, forgoing his usual singing; dressed, and went back into the bedroom feeling refreshed.

Louise soundly slept. Pierce smiled and scribbled a note explaining his whereabouts. He left the note on Louise's bedside table, air-kissed her goodbye, and headed to the office, stopping at a gas station to pick up a breakfast sandwich and coffee.

For two hours after arriving at the office, Pierce read criminal records, sorted through open-source information websites available to the public, and completed background checks on his people of interest. He rolled his shoulders back and forth, and his neck from side to side.

Better take a break.

At the coffee station, he poured his second cup of coffee and sipped it while sitting in his office chair, forcing himself to relax.

Break over, Pierce reached for the paperwork he had printed from the internet, and carefully reread his findings, underlining pertinent parts with a yellow marker.

Mace Leyton was born in 1954 in New York City's Grand Concourse section of the Bronx. Pierce could find no other New York City address for Mr. Leyton.

His background check revealed a 1973 petty larceny charge for the nineteen-year-old Mace Layton. He walked out of a supermarket in lower Manhattan without paying for $31.93 worth of groceries. Caught on camera, security held him until the police arrived. He was charged with a third-degree misdemeanor and sentenced to two-year's probation. On the address line of the arrest report, it said, 'Homeless.'

Pierce tapped his pen on the desk, wondering how long Mace had been homeless in Manhattan, and when he moved out of Rudolph's neighborhood.

Mace's employment history revealed a couple of supermarket jobs in Manhattan that didn't last long. He had many part-time jobs in the Bronx, New Jersey, and finally Pennsylvania until he landed at Coral Bells in 2002.

Pierce leaned back in his chair, mulling over Leyton's past.

After a moment, he ran his fingers through his hair and placed Mace's information aside. He then picked up another set of papers.

Grant Delacroix was born in the South Bronx in 1956. In 1974, he moved to Hyde Park, New York to attend culinary school. After graduating, he rented a small apartment in Poughkeepsie, where, after two years, he quickly worked his way up to sous chef at an Italian restaurant where he honed his culinary skills. In 1979, he landed in New York City at the famous Un Escargot French restaurant on the east side of Manhattan. He held the position of head chef at Un Escargot until 1999. In

2003, he moved to the Poconos. Coral Bells hired him the same year.

Pierce put down Grant's history and sat for a while, stroking his chin. Although no criminal record existed for the chef, Pierce was curious to know why Delacroix left a lucrative twenty-year career in New York City to accept a job in the Poconos. He could find no employment history for the chef between 1999 when he left Un Escargot and 2003 when he was hired at Coral Bells.

Did Delacroix run away from someone or something? And what was he doing between the time he left Un Escargot and when he started working at Coral Bells? Pierce wondered.

He scribbled on the chef's employment history, 'Why did Delacroix leave Un Escargot?'

Underlining the notation, he placed the information alongside Mace's. He then perused what he had gleaned from the internet for his other people of interest.

A phone call to Closed Doors, the agency that hired security guards for Coral Bells, confirmed Frank Irizarry's employment history. Before referring him to the security guard position at the residence, the agency had previously placed him at a couple of warehouse jobs during the past five years, with no complaints.

Josephine Devin's history with the agency was not as long as Frank's, but no complaints were filed in the four years she worked at Coral Bells. Jamie Alinsky retired from a thirty-year career as a dentist in 2001. Neither he, Frank, nor Josephine had criminal records. Of the three, only Alinsky had lived in Manhattan while attending the NYC College of Dentistry. They were all born and bred in Pennsylvania—Alinsky in Altoona, Josephine in Bethlehem, and Frank in Stroudsburg. If either of them had a grudge against Wane Rudolph, it had to have originated during Rudolph's short time at Coral Bells.

While Alinsky had reason to be upset when his bible class was appropriated by Rudolph, is that enough motive to kill him?

Pierce thought it unlikely that Alinsky or Irizarry had any involvement in Rudolph's death. Josephine, who looked to weigh all of one hundred five pounds, standing five feet three inches tall, in her employment picture, could not have overpowered Mr. Rudolph, regardless of his age.

Mace Leyton and Grant Delacroix both lived in the Bronx at the time of Ethan's suicide. Pierce eliminated everyone on his list but Leyton and Delacroix. He pondered his next move. The ringing telephone broke his concentration.

He checked his watch—8:35 a.m. Ruby wasn't due for another ten minutes. He was tempted to let the phone ring, but on the fourth ring, picked up.

"Pierce," he answered, annoyed. The telephone had interrupted his train of thought.

"Mr. Pierce. This is Father Carlway."

"Oh, yes, Father," he said, softening his tone. "Did you find anything on the Rudolphs?"

"Yes. Mr. and Mrs. Wane Rudolph were parishioners at St. Anthony's."

Pierce reached for a notepad and pen.

Instead of sharing what he had discovered, Father Carlway asked, "Would you be willing to come to St Anthony's and meet with Monsignor Sullivan? He was a young priest at the time of Ethan Rudolph's death, and remembers the family."

Surprised, Pierce dropped the pen. "Yes, of course," he answered, already dreading the long trip to the Bronx.

"Very well. How's tomorrow morning, at ten?"

Shit, I'll be caught in rush-hour traffic. "That's fine," he said.

"When you arrive at the rectory, ask for me. I'll introduce you to the monsignor. Do you need the address?"

"No Father. I'll find it. Thanks."

"See you then, Mr. Pierce."

"Goodbye, Father, and thank you for your help."

Pierce hung up the telephone and leaned back in his chair. If a meeting was required with someone familiar with the Rudolphs, there had to be something important better said in person. Rush-hour traffic or not, Pierce believed visiting the church would get him closer to unwinding the mystery of who killed Wane Rudolph.

Pierce hesitated, but with no other choice, he decided to roll the dice. He picked up the phone and dialed Frank's home number.

"Who is this?" Frank sounded hoarse from sleep and displeased the telephone had wakened him.

Shit. I forgot he works late.

"Frank, this is Howard Pierce. I'm sorry I woke you."

In an instant, Frank was fully awake, surprised, and thrilled when he heard Pierce's voice.

"Hi," he said as casually as he could. "I was just about to get up, anyway."

"I need you to do me a favor if you can," Pierce said.

"Anything." Frank threw off the bedcovers and sat up.

"I want you to ask Josephine if anyone came in before her shift ended on the morning of Mr. Rudolph's death."

"Sure. I can do that. I knew you were investigating a homicide," he said with certainty, hardly able to contain the excitement in his voice.

Pierce smiled despite himself. "Possible homicide, Frank."

"Yeah, sure."

"Please question Josephine without raising suspicions. Can I count on you to keep this confidential?"

"Yes, sir."

Pierce had been curious to see who showed up for Mr. Rudolph's funeral. Since he couldn't be in two places at once, he hoped Frank could handle it for him.

"One more thing, Frank. "Are you going to Mr. Rudolph's funeral tomorrow morning?"

"Yes. Do you want me to check out the mourners?" he asked enthusiastically.

"Yes, please. Look for anyone acting suspiciously, or, if you can, verify the identity of any stranger. Might be family from out of town. Mr. Miller said Mr. Rudolph's sister is flying in, but if any other stranger shows up, I want to know."

"I'll talk to Jo tonight soon as she comes in. Will it be too late to call you, or do you want me to wait 'till morning?"

Pierce shook his head. "You'll be at the funeral in the morning, Frank."

"Oh, yeah."

"In any case, I'll be out of town for most of the day. Call me right before you begin your shift tomorrow. I should be back by then."

"Will do."

"Goodbye, Frank, and thank you."

He hung up and smiled, imagining Frank doing the dance of joy. *He may turn out to be a good source, after all,* thought Pierce.

17

*H*oward Pierce arrived at St. Anthony's Church at nine-thirty but spent twenty minutes looking for parking. He finally maneuvered his Subaru into a tight spot three blocks away, hoping his PA license plate did not entice someone to break in.

Already pissed off at the traffic on Route 80, George Washington Bridge, and the Cross Bronx Expressway, he drew in a few deep breaths to calm himself before rushing to the church. He had to zigzag his way through the busy streets full of shoppers zipping in and out of grocery stores, picking through fruits and vegetables at outdoor stands, or pulling shopping carts behind them. A group of teens hanging outside a fast-food joint, munching on chicken and fries with greasy fingers, gave him the once over when he passed by. In that brief moment, Pierce had taken their measure and decided they posed no threat.

Outside the rectory, he glanced at his watch—9:55 a.m. He certainly would have been late if he hadn't tacked on an extra hour to his calculated drive time. As it is, he barely made it.

Pierce climbed the steps to the rectory and rang the doorbell, perspiring from the eighty-degree weather, his annoyance, and the crowded three-block walk.

A middle-aged woman wearing a flowery summer dress and pink sweater answered the door. In a slight Spanish accent, she asked, "Mr. Pierce?" her face showing uncertainty, despite expecting his visit.

Pierce nodded. "Yes, ma'am."

The woman smiled pleasantly enough and moved to the side. "Please come in. I'll ring Father Carlway for you." She gestured toward a worn wooden chair opposite her desk. "Please sit."

"Thank you."

The air had the welcomed chill and dusty scent of an overworked window unit, but Pierce didn't care. He breathed in the coolness and took the seat as she picked up the telephone.

"Father Carlway," she said. "Mr. Pierce is here to see you. Yes, Father." She hung up. "He'll be right down, Mr. Pierce."

Pierce glanced at the nameplate on her desk—Mrs. Ana Perez.

"Thank you, Mrs. Perez."

"You're welcome," she said and tapped on the typewriter keys while copying notes held up by a stand.

Pierce noticed her long, pink fingernails and the glint of her diamond wedding rings. He glanced around the room. Other than two file cabinets, shelves of books on everything from philosophy, mathematics, family dynamics, and matrimony to astronomy and Catholicism were displayed.

A minute later, Pierce heard footsteps coming downstairs, right outside the room. The door opened and a tall, lean man, dressed in black clerical garb, entered. "Mr. Pierce," he said, by way of introduction, "I'm Father Timothy Carlway. Thank you for coming."

Pierce stood to shake the proffered hand. "Nice to meet you, Father."

"I hope traffic wasn't too bad."

"It was fine," lied Pierce, ready to dispense with the niceties and get to the reason for the face-to-face.

"Good. If you'll follow me, Monsignor Sullivan is waiting for us."

Father Carlway led Pierce down a long, narrow corridor, where he stopped and knocked on Monsignor Sullivan's door.

"Come in," said a voice from within.

Holding the door ajar, Father Carlway motioned for Pierce to enter.

"May I present Mr. Howard Pierce?" he said, stepping inside the room.

Monsignor Sullivan wore a black cassock with purple buttons and stripes. He picked up his head from the papers he'd been reading and peered at them over his bifocals. With an air of a man used to wielding authority, he sat tall in his seat.

Pierce placed him to be in his late seventies or early eighties. The white hair made it difficult to tell since he's known people in their fifties with a full head of white hair. He glanced at the wall behind the priest. Not a Catholic, Pierce recognized the portrait of the pope but did not know the archbishop.

"Mr. Pierce, I apologize for asking you to come such a long way, but you'll understand why I thought it best to meet in person."

Eighty or not, the older man had a commanding voice, thought Pierce.

"No trouble at all, Monsignor," Pierce said.

"Please, take a seat. We have much to discuss."

"Thank you." Two seats were facing the desk. Pierce took the one directly in front of the monsignor.

"I'll leave you two to talk," said Father Carlway, silently closing the door behind him.

Without further preamble, Monsignor Sullivan picked up a sheet of paper and read.

Wane Rudolph and Lillian Carmen Marin, were married in

1954. Their son, Ethan Thomas Rudolph was baptized in 1955 when he was two months old. In 1962, he made Holy Communion at the age of seven.

Monsignor Sullivan cleared his throat.

In 1970, Ethan Thomas Rudolph passed away at fourteen years of age, halfway through his senior year in middle school.

THE REVEREND PUT down the paper and looked at Pierce. "After all these years, I can still see that sweet child tagging along with his parents even though one could see he didn't much care for the church." His lips chuckled, although his eyes were sad.

"Do you know what caused his death?" asked Pierce.

"Is that pertinent to your investigation?" snapped the reverend.

Unperturbed, Pierce said, "I'm aware Ethan died by suicide. What I'm asking is, how did he end his life?"

The monsignor's hooded eyes registered surprise.

Pierce added, "Knowing how he died might help me connect someone to him, possibly providing me with a motive for his father's murder."

"I see," said the cleric, his tone gentler. He inhaled through his nose and let it out slowly through his mouth. "Before I answer your question, let me say that the Church considers suicide to be a mortal sin, which, if the sinner does not repent, would lead to eternal damnation. Things have loosened up a bit, but there is no possible repentance in the case of suicide. You understand?"

Pierce nodded, unsure where this was heading.

"The boy drank a pint of whiskey with an almost full bottle of Prozac prescribed to Mrs. Rudolph for anxiety and depression."

Monsignor Sullivan fell silent, gaging Pierce's reaction.

When Pierce didn't react, he said, "Would you like a cup of coffee or tea? Perhaps water? On such a hot day, water might be more refreshing."

"Oh no, thank you, I'm fine," said Pierce.

"All right then."

Pierce noticed the priest's discomfort. To put him at ease, he asked, "How long have you been at St. Anthony's?"

"Since 1969. I was assigned to St. Anthony's after spending a year in a Brooklyn parish right out of the seminary. Barely a year later, I heard Mrs. Rudolph's confession a few days after the boy's funeral." He paused and took on a faraway look.

Pierce had seen that look before—someone conjuring an old memory from the recesses of the mind.

The monsignor said, almost in a whisper, "I remember Mrs. Rudolph being in a most agitated state. She confessed her son had committed suicide and it was she who found him when she went to wake him for school. Naturally, I felt for the bereaved mother. As gently as I could, I told her I would pray for the family. Believing suicide to be a mortal sin, I did not know how else to comfort her. But I understood Mrs. Rudolph had to tell someone how she found her boy and that somehow in the confessional, she would find absolution for her son. So I listened as she unburdened herself. After she recited the Act of Contrition, and I gave her my blessing, she did not attempt to leave. I asked her if there was something else troubling her. That's when she said she found a letter beside her dead son, addressed to her."

Pierce's pulse quickened. "He left a letter?"

The monsignor nodded. "Yes."

"Know what happened to it?" Pierce asked, hoping it still existed.

"I advised Mrs. Rudolph to give it to the police, but she adamantly refused, saying there were things her son had written she didn't want anyone to know, not even her husband. She asked if the Church would safeguard it in the archives, along with her son's history. Torn, she couldn't bear to keep it but did not know what else to do with the last words Ethan had written. I told her I couldn't do that, but she would not leave the confessional until I had promised to safeguard her son's last words. I had no choice but to agree. When I opened the door to the booth, she handed me an envelope containing the letter. I put it in my pocket, and after hearing the last confession for the day, I went directly to my room."

"Did you read the letter?" Pierce asked, hardly able to contain his curiosity.

The monsignor bowed his head.

Pierce thought he was probably considering how much he should tell him.

When he raised his head, he explained, "You have to understand, by accepting that letter I did something contrary to the Church's rules. I didn't know what to do. I knelt by my bed and prayed, but after asking God for guidance, I knew I couldn't let the monsignor see it. He would have ordered me to give it back to Mrs. Rudolph. And even though I didn't think it my place to read a personal message from a son to his mother, curiosity got the better of me, and I read it." He again bowed his head. We are all human, after all. Aren't we?"

"Yes Father," Pierce said.

"So, I did as Mrs. Rudolph asked and hid the letter in the archives. When Father Sullivan came to see me about your inquiry, I gave him permission to search the archives and bring Ethan's letter to me."

Pierce's heart skipped a beat.

The reverend stared beyond Pierce. Almost to himself, he said. "Today I again read the letter from that troubled young boy who could find no solution to his family situation, and it broke my heart all over again."

"May I please have a copy?" Pierce asked expectantly.

"Mrs. Rudolph passed away in 2005 so I don't think I would be breaking her trust if I gave you a copy. Ethan's letter may shed some light on the answers you seek." He reached for a folder. "I have prepared a file with all the information we have on the Rudolphs, including a copy of the letter, for you to take with you."

"I appreciate that."

Monsignor Sullivan offered the folder to Pierce, who reached for it, eager to get to that letter.

"May I ask why you saved it?"

"Compassion, Mr. Pierce. Regardless of the Church's strict rules, I couldn't deny Mrs. Rudolph's request." He shook his head, clearly burdened by the memory. "I commiserated with that poor mother, so I did as she asked and hid it in the archives. Perhaps if I'd been with the Church a while longer, I wouldn't have done it, but I was young and impetuous then." He smiled weakly.

Pierce stood. "It was a pleasure to meet with you, Monsignor. Thank you for your help."

Monsignor Sullivan reached across his desk to shake hands. "If you find the murderer, that will be thanks enough."

Pierce practically ran back to his car. Once inside, he turned the AC on full blast and dove into the letter, impatient to see what it would reveal.

18

When he first contacted Pierce, Frank had been sure Pierce would accept his help to be his inside man on the premises. But despite his disappointment when Pierce turned him down, Frank held onto the belief that his hero detective, experienced in solving homicides, had to have been called to investigate a murder no matter what he'd said about not being a homicide detective anymore. He was ecstatic when the former detective finally realized he needed him after all. After hanging up with Pierce, he began to strategize on the best way to question Josephine.

When she came in, Josephine found Frank slumped in the receptionist's chair. She wondered why he looked so pensive. Usually, he would be on the computer playing one of his silly video games with his Walkman tuned to the pop station.

"What's got you down?" she asked.

Frank sat up. "Hi, Jo. I'm all right. Just thinking." He got up to offer her the chair.

Josephine pulled out a drawer, dropped her purse into it, and closed it before sitting. "What has you thinking so hard, Frank?"

Frank leaned on the edge of the desk. "I can't stand this

weather. That rainstorm we had last week has done nothing to relieve this heat."

"Tell me about it," Josephine said, signing in.

"I love to sleep in when it's pouring rain. You?" asked Frank, grabbing the timesheet from her and initialing her time.

"Oh yeah. Nothing like a good rainstorm for sleeping."

Frank casually said, "It poured on the morning Mr. Rudolph died. Didn't it?"

Josephine scrunched her eyebrows. "What made you think of that?" she asked, stowing the timesheet in the drawer.

"That rain was a doozy, is all."

"Shit yeah. Cats and dogs."

"The people rushing to tend to Mr. Rudolph got here fast despite fighting the storm. I admire them for working in bad weather."

"Yeah, me too," Josephine said, wondering why Frank had brought up Mr. Rudolph's death.

"Rain makes me sleepy. I bet the residents slept in that morning," Frank said.

Josephine stared at Frank. "Hey, has Mr. Rudolph's death upset you so much you can't stop thinking about it? If so, you know you can talk to me."

"Well, it was pretty upsetting, but I'm all right, really, Jo. Thanks for your concern."

"Are you sure?"

"It's just that I worry about some of our older residents and hope none of them got caught up in that storm. I heard Mr. Montgomery skipped his tennis game two days in a row because he caught a cold."

"Oh, I'm sure he's fine, Frank. He and his wife seem pretty healthy."

"I know, but he may spread that cold around."

"Never figured you for a germaphobe," she said, reaching over and touching his arm.

"Who me? No." He waited a moment and said, "I can't imagine anyone other than the responders slogged their way in here that morning. You know how some of these folk are early risers who like to take walks in all kinds of weather."

"Only person who came in before Mr. Miller ran down like a madman was the chef," she said absentmindedly, opening the drawer to pull out a book from her purse.

"Delacroix?" asked Frank, as casually as he could.

"Yeah. He came in earlier than usual looking like a wet dog and carrying a box of donuts." She turned to Frank. "I kinda made fun of him," she laughed.

"Really?"

"Yeah. It's a miracle the donuts made it here intact. He was drenched. I grabbed the box and chose a coconut custard before he took them to the coffee room. While I looked over the donuts, he sneezed so loud he could've waken the dead," she laughed again.

"Wow," Frank laughed with her. "How early was that Jo?"

"I believe it was around six," she said, with tears in her eyes from laughing so hard.

Frank whistled. "Damn."

"I asked him what he was doing here so early. Said he couldn't sleep. Imagine? With all that wonderful rain, he couldn't sleep."

"Are you kidding me? I would've snored past my alarm clock."

Josephine said, "Me too." She picked up her latest love story, hoping Frank would get the hint and leave.

"Did he seem nervous or impatient while you decided on the donut?"

Josephine blew out her breath and put the book down. "I honestly didn't notice, Frank. Too busy deciding which donut to choose."

"Did the chef hang with you after you chose the donut?" asked Frank, ignoring her tone.

"Why are you asking so many questions? If you want to know why the chef was here so early, ask him," she said impatiently.

"Just chatting, Jo. No need to get upset."

"I'm sorry, Frank. I've been in a mood lately. It's this damn heat."

"It's okay."

"To answer your question, he picked up the box and left. Said he was going to get paper towels to wipe the foyer of the puddles he made when he came in, but he disappeared. I ended up doing it. Guess he wanted to get out of those wet clothes."

Frank straightened up and signed out. He'd gotten what he wanted. "Okay. I'm outta here. Have a good night, Jo. Enjoy your novel."

"Bye, Frank," she said, already opening the book.

Frank couldn't wait to tell Detective Piece the chef killed Mr. Rudolph. He hardly slept that night. In the morning, he dressed in his best suit and attended the funeral where he watched the chef who sat with Mace. *I'll prove my value, Detective Pierce!*

———

WHEN HE ARRIVED at his office after visiting with the monsignor, Pierce dashed up the stairs. Although eager to connect the dots between Rudolph's son and his prime suspect, he did not forego his ritual of touching the signage bearing his company name.

"Hi boss," greeted Ruby, coming away from the coffee machine after starting the brew cycle.

Pierce thought he'd seen all of Ruby's hairstyle changes during the two years she had been working for him, but he was wrong. Not only had Ruby forsaken the curls she claimed to have loved, but had her hair cut to within an inch of her scalp.

"Hi. I see you've cut your hair."

Ruby rubbed her head. "Yes, those curls were making me hot."

"I see," he said, noticing the knitted sweater she wore over her dress.

"It suits you."

Ruby smiled. Thanks. I saw a model in a magazine with this haircut and wondered how it would look on me, so I tried it. Glad you like it, but I'll probably let it grow out and try another look."

"Uh-huh."

Concerned the air in the office was too cold for his assistant, Pierce said, "Ruby, if you're cold, you can turn down the AC."

"I'm not cold," she said, contradicting her attire.

Pierce said, "Okay. Any messages?"

"Yes. a Mrs. Stetson called wanting to speak with you about surveilling her husband." I set up an appointment for her for tomorrow at three."

"Okay. Thanks, Ruby. If anybody else calls, say I'm out of the office and take a message, except for Frank Irizarry. Patch him in as soon as he calls."

"Sure thing, Boss. I take it your meeting with the priest went well?"

Pierce couldn't help but smile. "Yes. I'm almost ready to hand my investigation over to Detective Ramirez."

"That's great, boss."

"Thanks."

Before he walked away, he asked her, "Would you please pick up lunch for me? I'm starving."

Ruby glanced at her watch. "Almost two. No wonder you're starving. Anything, in particular, you'd like?"

"Grilled cheese on wheat and an iced tea is fine. Take the

money out of petty cash and get yourself something too," he said, already walking into his office.

Ruby reached for her office keys and unlocked her bottom desk drawer where she kept the petty cash box. She took out a few bills, locked the drawer, and took off her sweater, placing it over her chair back before leaving.

Pierce opened the file the monsignor had given him. He took out the letter and reviewed it, this time jotting down notes. That done, he relaxed into his chair and closed his eyes. The circumstantial evidence in Rudolph's apartment as described by Miller, is useless, thought Pierce. All such evidence no longer exists.

Ruby's knock interrupted Pierce's thought process. His eyes sprung open. "Come in."

Ruby entered with a bag in one hand and a drink in the other. She placed his lunch on his desk.

Pierce again eyed her buttoned-up sweater and said, "You didn't go out in that heatwave wearing your sweater, did you?"

She laughed. "No, of course not. I took it off before I left. Enjoy your lunch, and thanks for my chocolate shake."

"My pleasure, Ruby," said Pierce, shaking his head and watching her walk out and shut the door.

He immediately unwrapped his sandwich, again thinking of the circumstances of his investigation while he ate.

Mrs. Garcia's testimony that she saw someone at Rudolph's apartment would be contested, since she cannot identify who she saw, and no one could say if Rudolph expected him. Further, she did not see him break in. Since the cause of death was determined as a cardiac event, proving a case for homicide can only be proven by a confession from the murderer.

Pierce took the last bite of his sandwich and slurped the rest of his iced tea. He swiveled his chair and tossed the trash into the nearby basket. "Two points," he said.

Rolling his chair back, he picked up Delacroix's file. The note he had scribbled reminded him to call the chef's last employer in New York City. After looking up the number for Un Escargot, he dialed.

"May I speak with the owner, please," said Pierce when someone at the restaurant answered.

"May I ask what this is about?"

"My name is Howard Pierce. I'm a private investigator. I'm interested in the employment history of one of your former chefs who left your establishment in 1999.

"Chef Delacroix?" asked the woman on the phone.

"Yes ma'am."

"The chef worked here for many years. Grant was an excellent cook."

"Do you know why he left?"

There was silence on the other end of the line.

"Ma'am?" asked Pierce.

"I think you'd better speak with the owner about that. If you'll give me your number, I can have him call you back."

"All right. Thank you."

After leaving his number, Pierce went back to review the information he had gathered, highlighting the relevant information to build his case.

At precisely 3:45 p.m. the phone rang. Pierce had just finished arranging papers in two piles—one for his two suspects, and the other for the ones on both Ruby's and his list of people he eliminated. He was tired and wanted to take a nap in his chair, but when the phone rang, he immediately picked up, hoping Frank was on the other end.

"Pierce," he said

"Frank here."

"Yes, Frank. Got anything for me?"

"I'll say."

Pierce sat up.

"You're not going to believe who killed Mr. Rudolph."

"The chef," said Pierce.

"Ah, man. How did you know?" said Frank sounding like the air had just escaped out of his balloon.

"I figured it out, Frank. But I'm sure you have information to contribute. Tell me exactly what Josephine Devin told you."

Pierce grabbed his pen.

"Jo, I mean Josephine, said on the morning of Mr. Rudolph's death, the chef came in around six, soaking wet and carrying a box of donuts. In that rainstorm. Can you believe it?" He laughed. "Jo teased the chef about being wet."

Pierce wrote the time on his pad.

"Did she notice his state of mind?"

"Jo wasn't paying attention, as she was busy picking out a donut. She chose a coconut custard. Good choice."

Pierce rolled his eyes. "How long was he by her desk?"

"I can't imagine no more than five minutes, because Jo said after she chose her donut, he picked up the box and left."

Pierce again wrote on his pad.

"Good job, Frank. Thanks for talking to her."

"One more thing. Jo said while she was trying to decide on the donut, he sneezed."

Pierce's eyes widened. "Sneezed?"

"Yes, so loud he could've waken the dead, is how she put it." Frank snickered.

Pierce scribbled, 'Chef and the mystery man both sneezed noisily.'

"By the way, if by chance it turns out the chef did not kill Mr. Rudolph," said Frank. "I think you should look at the handyman. I checked out his workroom and found a locksmith kit with all kinds of key-making tools."

"How did you get into the workroom? Isn't it locked?"

"Well, yeah, but I took the code off the padlock and had a key made. Told the locksmith I'd lost my key. After taking down my identification and verifying I worked at Coral Bells, he made a key for me."

Clever.

"You're aware that's breaking and entering, right, Frank?"

"I know," he said, sheepishly."

Pierce let him stew for a moment. "Go on."

Frank came alive again. "I thought I'd hit the jackpot, but then I thought, why would Mace need to make keys when he already has master keys?"

"Makes sense," said Pierce.

"Anyway, Mace may not have used a key to get to Mr. Rudolph, but I still think he could've done it."

"What makes you think so?"

"Have you seen the size of him? If anyone could take somebody down, it would be him. Come to think of it, Grant is pretty big himself, and those massive hands on them both?"

Of course, thought Pierce.

"In my opinion, they're both strong candidates for murder, is all I'm saying," said Frank. And there's something else."

"What?"

"While nosing around in the workroom, I found a note carelessly thrown on the floor. Someone was looking forward to a weekly card game after closing up. I think the chef wrote it."

"Why do you think so?"

"They signed it G, for Grant. Don't you think?"

"Maybe. Did you keep the note?"

"I sure did."

"Do you have access to a fax?"

"Yeah. There's one in the management office."

"Okay. Please fax it to me at the same office number except for the last digit. It's a nine."

"Will do."

"Who attended the funeral?"

"Well, there was Mr. Miller, of course. He was inconsolable, and a few residents were there. An old woman, someone identified as Mr. Rudolph's sister, sat still and silent in the first pew, dressed in one of those scary horror movie getups with a veil covering her face. Gave me the creeps."

Pierce shook his head, smiling. "Anyone else, Frank?"

"Mace Leyton and Grant Delacroix attended the service, as well as a couple of other staff members. Mace was the first to arrive. When Grant showed up, he waved him over. They sat together but I noticed they were both silent throughout the service. Maybe they argued. Perhaps about the murder?"

Pierce had to herd Frank in when he went off-topic. "Exactly who among the residents and staff attended, Frank?"

"Grace Johnson was first to arrive. She sat in the front pew. Have you met her?"

"I have."

"She's the so-called mayor. Of course, she sat up front." He scoffed.

"Who else was there, Frank?"

"From the bible studies class, Jamie Alinsky, Alison Johns, Fred Cross, and Amy Davis. Mrs. Garcia was there too. "Oh, and Mrs. Lee, but she was in a wheelchair, so I don't think she could've done it," he said, again laughing. "No one else showed."

Pierce wrote their names as Frank recited them.

"Notice anything out of the ordinary?" asked Pierce.

"I was getting to that."

"I'm listening."

"I watched Mace and Grant carefully. They being our prime suspects," he chuckled.

"Did you overhear what they were saying?"

"Nah. I wanted to sit behind them so I could listen, but Mrs. Garcia and Mrs. Johnson beat me to it, and I didn't want to sit next to the creepy woman in black."

Pierce shook his head.

"I had no choice but to sit two rows back, but I kept my eyes on them," Frank said. "During prayers neither of them bowed their heads or kneel when the others did. Guess they're not religious. Anyway, while they carried the casket out to the limo, everyone stood and turned to follow the procession out the door. That's when I saw Grant's jaw tighten and his fists curl into a ball. I swear the dude was tense. Service over, he hurried out and drove away. Mace hung around talking to the mourners."

"Thank you for the information, Frank. I appreciate your help."

"Hey. I was going to the funeral, anyway."

"Talk to you soon, Frank."

Pierce thought about Frank's observations. It added weight to his assessment implicating the chef as the murderer. All the pieces he needed to present his findings to Sergeant Ramirez were there. He went over his main points.

One. Chef Grant Delacroix lived in Rudolph's neighborhood at the time of Ethan's death.

Two. Josephine Devin, the security guard on duty on the morning of Rudolph's death, said Delacroix arrived at Coral Bells at about six a.m. drenched from the rain. That explains the wet floor in Rudolph's apartment.

Three. Mrs. Garcia saw someone outside Rudolph's apartment sixteen minutes after six. Both she and Josephine Devin mentioned the sneeze.

Four. The pathologist report listed the time of death between six-thirty and seven-thirty.

The timeline is solid, although not conclusive, thought Pierce. *Ethan's letter is the clincher. It doesn't prove Delacroix murdered Ethan's father decades later, but it's enough for the police to question him.*

Pierce shoved all the information he had on Delacroix into his briefcase. The telephone rang.

"Pierce."

This is Marvin Gladstone of Un Escargot. I understand you seek information on Grant Delacroix?"

"Yes, Mr. Gladstone. Thank you for calling me back."

"I don't normally give out employee info on the telephone, but I checked your website. Your background as a decorated homicide detective convinced me to call."

"I appreciate that."

"How may I help you? I hope Grant was not the victim of a homicide."

"No, sir. I'd like to know the reason the chef left your employ after twenty years."

"I fired him for being drunk and disorderly."

"Surely that wasn't the first time he'd been drunk on the job?"

"Please understand, Chef Delacroix was an excellent chef. The restaurant owes a lot of our success to his culinary skills. As long as he performed, and didn't upset the customers, I turned a blind eye to his drinking. You could say he was a functioning alcoholic. I tried talking to him about getting help, but he assured me he had it under control, and frankly, he did."

"What happened on the day you fired him?"

"I was at the front of the house greeting our dinner guests when a commotion coming from the kitchen turned everyone's heads toward the noise. You can imagine my concern, not to mention embarrassment. Anyway, I rushed into the kitchen and the first thing I saw was the chef holding a pot over one of the workers, who was cowering on the floor covered in gravy. The kitchen staff stood at their stations as if frozen. I immediately pushed Grant away from Samuel and grabbed the pot out of the chef's hands."

"Was anyone else assaulted?"

"No, thank goodness. I asked the sous chef to finish service and ordered Grant to go through the kitchen's back entrance straight to my office. I had a restaurant full of people and had to first face them before dealing with Grant. After I assured all was well in the kitchen, that it was only a minor mishap, everyone went back to enjoying their dinners."

"Did the chef explain why he reacted the way he did?"

"Not to my satisfaction. He said something to the effect that the gravy looked lumpy to him and when he was contradicted, he blew up. Said he didn't realize he'd picked up the pot and poured the gravy over Samuel's head. He'd always been mercurial, but had never done anything like that."

"Was he intoxicated?"

"Oh yeah. I fired him on the spot, fearing a lawsuit."

Although he hadn't found any criminal activity in Delacroix's history, Pierce asked, "Did Samuel sue or bring up assault charges?"

Samuel is the son of one of my investors. After meeting with him, he agreed the negative publicity wouldn't do the restaurant any good. I gave Samuel a hefty bonus and settled the matter."

"I can understand that. One more thing. Chef Delacroix found employment in Pennsylvania three years after he left your restaurant. Any idea what happened to him after you fired him?"

"I heard he bummed around for a while. Someone saw him down at the Bowery, begging for change. Such a shame. But if he's cooking again, I hope he got his act together and is doing well."

"Thank you, Mr. Gladstone. You've been extremely helpful."

"You're welcome. Good luck with your investigation."

"Thanks."

Pierce remembered the chef's minty breath when he first met him at the restaurant. Perhaps he's still drinking, and he chews on mints to cover the odor.

The fax machine hummed. Pierce turned and grabbed the copy of the note Frank found in Mace's workroom. He glanced at it and shoved it in Delacroix's file even though he thought the note irrelevant.

19

First thing the next morning, Pierce picked up the phone. Detective Sergeant Ignacio Ramirez answered on the first ring. "SARP, Detective Ramirez speaking."

"Iggy. Howard here."

"Hey. What's up? Have you solved the mysterious case of death by natural causes yet?" he said, chuckling.

Pierce laughed. "Funny, Iggy."

"Seriously, have you concluded that we have a homicide on our hands?"

"I have."

"Son of a bitch! I knew I put the right man on the job."

"Thanks, pal, but it's going to be hard to prove unless the killer confesses, and that's where you come in."

"I'm listening."

"I'll need to show you the information I have on the suspect. Can you see me at the station?"

"When? Now?"

"The sooner the better."

"All right. Come on over. Don't know where I'll be later."

"On my way."

Pierce gathered what he had on Delacroix, along with the folder Monsignor Sullivan had given him, and rushed out the door.

When he passed her desk, he said to Ruby, "Please cancel all my appointments for today. I'll be at the precinct if you need me."

———

PIERCE HADN'T BEEN to the police station since his retirement. If he drove past Dey Street, he fought the urge to walk in and chat with the guys about their latest cases. He learned his lesson soon after his retirement when he'd call his former team to ask about their homicide cases and give unsolicited advice. No one wanted to talk shop with the ex.

Walking through the busy squad room, Pierce noticed a couple of unknown faces busy on the phone or filling out reports. A woman, clearly distressed, sat by one of the unfamiliar detectives. Passing by Pierce overheard the concern in her voice. "He hasn't come home …"

Pierce almost made it to his former office when a loud voice rang out, "Sarge!" Heads snapped up.

He recognized the voice and turned around.

A former team member rushed up to him and grabbed him in a bear hug, almost knocking him to the floor and dropping his briefcase.

"Nice to see you too, Jun," Pierce said, pulling away from him.

"What brings you here, Sarge? Everything okay?"

"Yeah. Everything's great. Just came by to see Iggy about something I'm working on."

"Something?" Detective Leung asked, tilting his head to the side.

"Well, more of an investigation I'm helping him with."

Sergeant Ramirez had been watching out for Pierce through his office blinds. He gave them a couple of minutes to greet each other, but knowing Leung, Ramirez didn't want Pierce to be caught up in a long conversation. He opened the door.

"Leung," he yelled. "You can catch up later. Pierce and I have business to discuss."

"Sure, Sarge," Leung said.

"If I'm around when you finish with Iggy, come by my desk," he said. "I'd love to hear what you've been up to."

"Sure will, Jun. Good to see you."

Sargent Ramirez closed the door behind them and motioned for Pierce to sit. "Lay it out for me, Howard," he said, plopping down on his chair.

Pierce put his briefcase on the desk and unlatched it. He took out a folder and placed it in front of Ramirez, closing the briefcase before pulling out a chair. "This is all the information I've been able to gather for Mr. Grant Delacroix, the chef at Coral Bells Adult Living apartments. They found no murder weapon at the scene, but I have a theory."

"Which is?" asked Ramirez, reaching for the file.

"When I examined Mr. Rudolph's body, his face had bruises around his nose, mouth, and chin. When they discovered the body, Rudolph wore a CPAP mask covering the same area. It's possible Delacroix held him down by pushing on the mask until Rudolph had a heart attack and died. Built like a linebacker, the chef is pure muscle with the largest hands I've ever seen. The victim was obese and in poor health, no match for a man the size of Delacroix."

"Hmm," Ramirez said, confident in his former boss's ability to build a case for murder from a small thing like someone having large hands.

Pierce continued. "Delacroix grew up in the same neighborhood as the Rudolphs, connecting him to the family." He pointed to the file. "In the folder is a copy of a letter given to me by Monsignor Sullivan, who knew the Rudolphs when they lived in the Bronx. The Rudolphs' only son, Ethan, left it for his mother to find before committing suicide."

"Does the letter implicate Delacroix in any way?" asked Ramirez.

"Not exactly, but Ethan mentions him by his first name."

"Hmm," said Iggy.

"Ethan wrote of his father's disapproval of how much time he spent with Grant, his father's constant criticism, and the derogatory names Rudolph called him. He also mentions his father's constant preaching and how he abused his mother."

"So he had a shit father. Doesn't prove motive for murder, Howard."

"No, but the information I've gathered points to Grant Delacroix."

"Okay. Go on."

"The monsignor said Mrs. Rudolph did not want her husband to see the letter."

"That's odd. Know why?"

"I think even though Delacroix bullied both Ethan and Mrs. Rudolph, she probably did not want him to blame himself for their son's death. I tell you, Iggy, I will never understand how a woman can live with a man who abuses not only her but her child and then spare him pain."

"Happens all the time, Howard. You and I have both inter-viewed women in a hospital put there by their husbands, who refuse to press charges."

Pierce nodded. "Yeah, I know, it's complicated, as they say."

"That it is, my friend. Tell me, how did the boy die?"

"Ethan's mother suffered from depression and anxiety. He ended his life ingesting his mother's Prozac, washing the pills down with his father's whiskey."

"Anything else?"

"I'm certain Grant was aware of Ethan's family situation.

According to the letter, Ethan had no one else to confide in. There certainly are enough reasons in that letter for Ethan's childhood friend to have avenged him, even if it took decades to do so."

Ramirez tapped his fingers on the file folder. "Have you interviewed anyone who can implicate Delacroix for the murder?"

"As you know, I interviewed Mr. Miller, who first brought his suspicions to the department. He introduced me to Mrs. Garcia, who, on the morning of Rudolph's death, heard someone sneeze outside of her apartment. She looked through the peephole and saw a man in front of Rudolph's door. Also, that morning, Delacroix came in earlier than usual. He sneezed in front of the security guard. The timeline fits from his entering the building to Mrs. Garcia seeing someone standing outside Rudolph's apartment, to time of death. Along with other circumstantial evidence as outlined in my summary, I believe we have enough to bring Delacroix in for questioning. It all fits, Iggy."

"All right," said Ramirez. "Let me read through all of this. Why don't you go visit with Leung? I'll call you when I'm done."

Pierce pushed his chair back and stood. "Thanks, Iggy."

Ramirez chuckled. "No, thank you for bringing me more work."

"Always happy to oblige."

"Get outta here and shut the door behind you."

A big smile crossed Pierce's face when he saw her at Leung's desk. "Ceci! It's good to see you," he said, walking toward her.

Detective Celia Byrne, a squad member under Pierce when he ran the unit, sprung from her seat and gave Pierce a tight hug. "How are you, Sarge? It's great to see you."

"Good, and you?"

"Oh, you know, living the dream." She tossed back her long hair.

Pierce smiled at the gesture he remembered so well.

"Sorry, I can't stay and talk. I'm about to head out. Maybe I can get the boys together and we can all have a drink soon."

"That'll be great."

"See ya later, Leung. Bye Sarge," she said and hurried out.

"Sit, Sarge," Leung said.

"Ceci looks good," Pierce said.

"Yeah, she always looks good."

"Yes. Is O'Malley or Hanley expected today? I'd like to say hi."

"Hanley transferred out last year. He's working in Philly now. O'Malley's out on medical."

"What happened to him?" Pierce asked, concerned.

"Suffered a mild heart attack."

"Oh no."

"Don't worry. He'd just gotten into the unmarked when it happened. Manny, our newest member, was with him and called for help."

"Is he going to be all right?" asked Pierce.

"Yeah. You know Sean. He'll bounce back. Maybe now he'll lay off all that junk food he eats." Leung chuckled.

"He still have the same home number?"

"Yeah."

"I'll give him a call."

"So tell me," asked Leung, leaning over his desk conspiratorially, "how's the PI business treating you?"

"Business is good, but I do miss Homicide."

"I can understand that." He sat up. "Listen, if you ever need me for anything, anything at all, ring me up, especially if you need help to identify old weapons."

"Jun, you'd be the only one I'd call for weapons' advice."

"Maybe you'll get a case like the last one we worked on. That gun was a beauty."

"It certainly was interesting."

"I mean it," said Jun. "Call me for anything you need. Got a card on you I can have?"

Pierce pulled out his business card from his wallet and gave one to Leung.

Leung studied the card. "Shit. Bloodhound Investigations." He doubled over in laughter.

"A little decorum, Leung," yelled a face Pierce did not recognize.

"Yeah, yeah," he said, wiping his eyes. "You named the agency after what that bitch called you? Genius!"

Pierce laughed. I couldn't let a good name go to waste, now could I?"

"No way."

The phone rang. Leung picked up. "SARP. Detective Leung speaking." He picked up a pencil and scribbled something on a notepad. "All right," he said and hung up.

"Gotta go. It was great seeing you, Sarge. Keep in touch."

"I will," said Pierce.

Leung walked out of the squad room.

Pierce looked around at the busy room, missing the hustle and bustle that was his life for so many years. A couple of minutes later, Ramirez opened his door and called out, "Pierce."

"What a sad letter that boy left," he said as soon as Pierce entered the room.

Pierce nodded.

"You've convinced me, Howard. Even though the evidence is circumstantial and here- say, there's enough here to bring in Mr. Delacroix for questioning. Gonna have to lean on him hard if we're to get a confession, though."

"How soon can you arrange it?"

"I can have him picked up within the hour."

"That's great, Pierce said with an expectant look on his face."

"Howard, you know I can't let you into the interview room,

but would you like to wear an earpiece so you can communicate with me from the other side of the glass?"

Pierce had hoped Ramirez would invite him to watch the interrogation. Giving him an earpiece would allow him to talk to Ramirez, perhaps suggesting a question or two to pose to the suspect. "You bet," he said.

"Thought you'd like that."

"Iggy, I understand it's not kosher to allow a private citizen, which I am, to be a witness while questioning a suspect. I appreciate you making an exception."

"Please, you did the legwork. I'm just the mouthpiece, but please don't come barging in if things go south," he laughed.

"I won't."

"And let's keep it to ourselves for obvious legal reasons."

"Of course."

Ramirez picked up the phone. "Manny, pick up Chef Grant Delacroix at Coral Bells Adult Living apartments for questioning in the matter of Wane Rudolph's death and take Seale with you."

"Let's go around the corner and grab a proper cup of coffee," he said to Pierce, hanging up.

20

*T*he morning after the murder, Grant Delacroix tossed and turned in his drunken stupor. Murky images of Wane Rudolph's eyes as he snuffed out his life caused him to moan in his sleep.

But the nightmares didn't start with the murder. They had become a problem weeks before when Grant passed by the game room on a quick break before dinner service. He stopped cold when he heard his voice, "Come to papa." Grant thought his ears deceived him, but the man again spoke. "That's twice I beat you."

A shudder gripped Grant's entire body when he looked inside the room. Although older and fatter, there was no mistaking the arrogant air Rudolph had about him as he collected his winnings. He wanted to grab the old man and beat the shit out of him right then and there. Instead, he quickly ambled away. That day, the chef could barely concentrate on his duties, snapping at his staff more than usual. He rushed to the nearest liquor store on his way home, where he guzzled down a pint of whiskey, breaking his six-year sobriety record. At first, he only drank after work, but soon found he needed that morning drink to calm the jitters.

Although used to the chef's outbursts, his staff couldn't help but notice he had become more confrontational than ever frequently blowing bibulous breaths into people's faces. When he greeted his diners, however, Grant put on a fake smile and performed his usual celebrity act, posturing like a peacock for his adoring fans.

The sound of his excruciatingly loud alarm clock penetrated his nightmare, and he abruptly sat up in bed, triggering a headache. The buzzing of the alarm felt like hammers pounding the inside of his head. He moaned and reached over to slam his hand over the alarm's off button. Swinging his legs over the edge of the bed, he slowly rose, instantly feeling sick. He stumbled into the bathroom, barely making it to the toilet, where he dropped to the floor and retched. After standing under the cool shower for twenty minutes, his head cleared. Feeling somewhat human, he stepped out of the shower and shaved. Downing a couple of aspirins with a cup of strong coffee, the chef was ready to perform.

The restaurant was full for a celebratory fiftieth wedding anniversary brunch. Chef Delacroix had made it in without a minute to spare. Because he was short-staffed, he was at the pass checking orders and expediting, when his maître 'd, reluctant to disturb him on such a busy day, approached.

"Excuse me, chef," said the head waiter.

The chef, without breaking his stride, sarcastically said, "What is it? Someone didn't like their soufflé?"

"No, Chef." The maître d' lowered his voice. "I mean, there are two detectives here to see you."

Delacroix's stomach tightened. His first instinct was to run, but accustomed to hiding his feelings, he said, "One moment," and called out to one of the cooks at the meat station. "Roger, let Maggie do that. Get over here and take over."

The two officers patiently stood by.

Roger signaled to Maggie at the meat station and rushed to the pass.

"Make sure you don't fuck it up."

"Yes, Chef," Roger said.

De Lacroix then faced the officers, and with a calm, he did not feel, politely asked, "How may I help you, gentlemen?"

The burlier of the two spoke. "This is Detective Seale. I'm Detective Morse. We'd like you to come with us to the station to answer a few questions."

Delacroix donned his best smile and said, "Questions regarding what, may I ask?"

"We're investigating the death of Mr. Wane Rudolph and want you to clear up a few things for us."

A collective gasp from the kitchen staff provoked an angry response from the chef.

He bellowed, "Don't you people have work to do?"

"Yes, Chef," responded all.

"Then get to it and mind your own business."

He addressed the detectives. "Didn't Mr. Rudolph die of a heart attack?"

"There are some loose ends we'd like to tidy up," said Morse with a serious face. "We're hoping you can clear up a few things for us."

Grant said, "Can it wait, gentlemen? I would be happy to go to the station to answer questions when the rush dies down. As you can see, we are busy." He smiled. "We're preparing a special brunch for a couple celebrating their fiftieth anniversary, bless their hearts."

"We'd appreciate it if you would come with us now, sir," said Detective Seale, who looked ready to cuff him if Delacroix refused to comply.

Grant clicked his tongue. "Even though it's inconvenient, I'd be happy to cooperate in any way I can, detectives. Lead the way."

"After you said Detective Morse, extending his hand toward the doors.

Aware of the whispers and questioning stares as he walked out of the kitchen and into the dining room, followed by two men, Delacroix did not lose his cool. His straight back and the way he met everyone's gaze with that million-dollar smile of his exuded confidence.

Trying to convey a sense of normalcy, the chef strode over to the couple whose long marriage inspired the shindig. Seale and Morse looked at each other, prepared for any desperate move the suspect might make.

The couple smiled when the chef bowed, took the hand of the missus, and said, "Happy anniversary. I hope everything will be to your satisfaction."

The woman beamed, as did her husband. Delacroix then kissed her hand and reached over to shake his. "Thank you, Chef," said the husband. The restaurant exploded in applause, everyone standing. Chef Delacroix strolled out. Seale and Morse looked at each other, amazed at the man's magnetism.

Grace Johnson, who sat a few tables over from the couple, couldn't resist following them out the door, hoping to overhear why the chef was being led out by the men she had already determined were police officers. When they passed the lobby, the few residents there took up the same whispered conversations now going on in the restaurant.

Monica stared when they passed by her desk and out the door. She had directed the detectives to the restaurant, wondering what was happening there. When she saw Grace trailing them out the door, she knew she'd get the scoop from her.

Monica was right. Grace came back looking like the cat who

swallowed the canary. "Grace," Monica said, stopping her from passing by. "Do you know what that was about?"

Grace bent down and whispered, "I believe they have implicated our chef in the death of Mr. Wane Rudolph."

Monica gasped.

With a glint in her eye, Grace elaborated. "When one of the officers opened the car door for the chef, he complained he felt like a criminal in front of his staff and his patrons. The officers remained stone-faced, which made the chef angry. He then said, mind you, in a most controlled voice, even though I could tell he wanted to yell, 'I don't know anything about Mr. Rudolph's death.' The chef claimed he didn't see why he had to be escorted to the police station in front of his patrons. They then thanked him for his cooperation and held the car door open for him." She giggled. "The chef then got in the car in a huff."

Monica was stunned. "No. That can't be. Mr. Rudolph had a heart attack and died."

"Oh you innocent child," said Grace. "From the first moment, that man, ah, Mr. Martal started asking questions, I suspected he was here undercover."

"I can't believe it," Monica said, astonished.

"You'll see. Anyway, I gotta get back. See ya later." She almost ran to the restaurant to spread the news.

During the short ride to the station, Grant wondered how the police could have connected him to Rudolph's murder. He'd been careful not to leave incriminating evidence. *What made them suspicious Rudolph didn't die of a heart attack? Are they questioning everyone at the residence? No, I would have heard about it in that gossip-ridden place. They must have something on me.* Stomach in knots, nerves frayed, yearning for a drink, he willed himself to remain calm.

Arriving at the station, Grant De LaCroix walked in poised and ready to cooperate as any citizen would do.

21

Grant Delacroix's eyes flitted around the windowless, austere room. He'd been waiting for ten minutes, which felt like an hour to him. The bolted bar on the table, tape recorder, and large mirror almost cracked the cemented smile he stubbornly held. Grant suspected he was being watched when he saw the mirror and was determined not to appear nervous.

Sargent Ramirez and Pierce did indeed watch him. "Better get started. If he keeps smiling like that, we might have to call a doctor to set his face back to normal," joked Pierce.

Ramirez laughed. "Yeah."

"Good luck," said Pierce.

Sergeant Ignacio Ramirez, carrying a folder, inserted the earpiece in his left ear before entering the room. He walked past Delacroix, dropped the folder on the table, and pulled out a chair.

"Thank you for coming in. I know how busy you are. Would you like a cold drink, or perhaps a cup of coffee?"

What Grant desired was a shot of whiskey. "No thank you,"

he said, folding his hands atop the table to keep them from shaking. "Is this going to take long? I need to get back to the restaurant," he said, trying to modulate his voice to hide his nervousness.

"That depends on you," said Ramirez.

De Lacroix blinked.

Ramirez clicked on the tape recorder. "Let's begin."

"Is that necessary?" asked De Lacroix, anxiously staring at the machine.

"Standard procedure. Ignore it."

For the benefit of the recording, Sergeant Ramirez stated, "Interview with Chef Grant Delacroix in the matter of Wane Rudolph's investigation," He looked at his watch, "eleven-o-nine a.m. September 3, 2007."

Delacroix clenched his jaw at the mention of Wane Rudolph's name.

Pierce's voice came in crystal clear through Ramirez's earpiece. *Notice his reaction to the name Wane Rudolph?*

Ramirez slightly bowed his head.

"Tell me," Ramirez said in his friendliest voice, "How long have you been a chef?"

Grant tore his eyes away from the tape recorder. He cleared his throat. "Over twenty-five years."

Ramirez whistled. "Long career. Go to culinary school?"

Delacroix willed himself to appear cooperative but bored. He unfolded his hands and tried to look comfortable in the hard metal chair. "Yes, in upstate New York."

"Long way from the Poconos. Did you live in New York City before moving upstate?"

"I was born in the Bronx," he casually said. "When I graduated high school, I moved to Hyde Park to attend culinary school."

"Where in the Bronx did you live before moving?"

"Melrose."

Ramirez tapped his fingers on the folder but did not flip it open.

The earpiece came alive again. *Find out what he did after leaving Un Escargot until he came to Coral Bells.*

"Why did you leave Un Escargot after twenty years?"

Grant lost his composure and erupted. He sat up. "What's with all these personal questions? Did you run a background check on me?" he asked, knowing the answer.

"Calm down Mr. Delacroix," warned Ramirez.

Grant slowly inhaled and exhaled. "What does my employment history have to do with why I'm here?"

Ramirez leaned forward and firmly said, "It's all part of our investigation. If you've nothing to hide, a question about your background shouldn't be a big deal."

De LaCroix ran his fingers across his forehead, coming away with perspiration. He casually ran his hand across his pants leg, trying to regain control of his emotions.

"I don't understand," he said. "What difference does it make where I worked or where I lived when I was a kid?"

"If you'll just answer the questions, we can get through this as quickly as possible."

Delacroix's jaw tightened and he said, "All right. Get on with it, then."

Ramirez relaxed.

Thought I was going to have to send the calvary in there.

Ramirez almost smiled at Pierce's humor.

He asked again. "Why'd you leave Un Escargot?"

Delacroix didn't want to admit they had fired him, but sensed Ramirez already had the answers to his questions. He looked away, the memory still stinging. "They fired me for drinking on the job and assaulting one of my kitchen staff."

"Is that when you moved out of New York?"

The chef looked surprised Ramirez hadn't asked him to elaborate on the assault. "No. After bumming around for a while, I met someone who convinced me to attend an AA meeting. By that time, I had pissed away my savings and was about to be evicted. I realized I didn't want to live on the streets, so I joined AA and got sober, but word had gotten around about my drinking, and no one would hire me. After a year of trying, I gave up."

Ask him if he ever considered working as a short order or line cook. Bet that'll get a reaction from the arrogant chef.

"Why didn't you look for a job as a short-order cook or line cook somewhere until you got your shit together?"

The question made Delacroix's face flush red. "Are you kidding me? I didn't go to culinary school to work in some dive."

"No, of course not."

The nerve of you, Iggy.

"It's to your credit you got sober. Congratulations."

"Now that you know my story, can we wrap this up? I've got to get back to the restaurant."

Ramirez ignored him. "They say faith has a lot to do with the things one can overcome. Are you a religious man?"

"You're going to keep asking about my life, aren't you?"

"Look," Ramirez said, raising his voice, "How many times do I have to explain these questions are part of our investigation? Now, please answer the question."

Ramirez noticed the veins on the chef's temples throbbing.

After glaring at Ramirez for a moment, he gave up. "As a kid, I went to church because my mother made me, okay? But I never bought into all that religious mumble jumble."

"Was it St. Anthony's your family attended?"

With each question the detective asked, Delacroix's stomach churned until he thought he was going to be sick. It was obvious the police had done their homework. They had all the answers. "Yes. St. Anthony's," he said.

"Do you remember a Father Sullivan? Gave catechism classes back then."

"Vaguely."

Time to lower the boom, Iggy.

"We have every reason to believe Mr. Wane Rudolph was the victim of a homicide."

Ramirez and Pierce studied the chef carefully for his reaction.

Delacroix took in a breath, once again putting on an act, and sadly shook his head. Allowing himself a few seconds to calm his jittery stomach, but failing to keep the insincerity out of his voice, he said, "Oh my God. What makes you think someone murdered him? I thought he died from a heart attack."

"We'll get to that."

Ramirez flipped open the folder and picked up a sheet of paper, dropping the flap closed.

He took a few seconds, pretending to read over the paper. Delacroix's legs bounced under the table.

When Ramirez thought enough time had gone by, he looked directly into Grant's eyes and lowered the boom.

"Does the name Ethan Rudolph mean anything to you?"

The shock of hearing Ethan's name spoken out loud brought unexpected tears to Grant's eyes. He tried to speak, but his throat clogged. Memories of his childhood flooded his brain.

————

AN INTROVERTED, only child, who followed his mother around like a shadow, Grant found it hard to make friends. His parents struggled to keep their ethnic French cuisine restaurant from going under in a predominantly Hispanic neighborhood. Delacroix's mother did all the cooking while his dad tended tables and kept a watchful eye on the finances. Although Grant hated the kitchen where he did everything from washing dishes, and throwing out the trash, to prepping vegetables, he admired his parents for persevering. Eventually, word of mouth filled the seats, and the family settled into a comfortable living. Grant found it ironic he ended up a chef when all he wanted to do was get as far away from cooking as possible.

But as so often happens in life, Grant's love of cooking sparked, not in his mother's kitchen, but after a chance encounter on the Third Avenue El, one sweltering summer day.

The slow-moving fan blades of that packed subway car did little to relieve the oppressive heat saturating Grant's shirt with sweat, exacerbated by the two large people sitting on opposite sides of him.

Wiping beads of perspiration from his forehead with the back of his clammy hand as the train came to a stop, he took in a breath when, along with most of the other passengers, the adults sandwiching him, stood to leave.

Grant now had a clear view of a boy sitting across from him, reading a book. He wondered how someone could be so cool in the hot subway car, with not a bead of sweat on his brow, nor damp strands of long hair stuck to his face. Even his neatly pressed polo shirt and khaki pants had not a stain on them. Grant couldn't help but stare from the boy's head to his Converse sneakers, which, although worn, looked cleaner than they had a right to.

When the boy looked up from his book to check the approaching station, Grant twisted his head toward the window. It took all his concentration to focus on the passing city land-scape, as if it intrigued him. Every so often, he dared a glimpse at the young man who had gone back to reading his book.

When the Claremont Parkway station came into view, they both rose, prepared to leave the train. "Hi," said the stranger unexpectedly as they walked down the stairs and onto the side-walk. Grant flinched. "Hi," he nervously said.

"I've seen you on this train before."

Grant was stunned. He certainly had never seen *him* before.

"I'm Ethan."

Grant swallowed hard, but could not speak. He felt sweat trickle down the sides of his forehead and onto his face. A drop of sweat fell from his nose before Grant could swat it away.

Ethan smiled. "Got a name?" he asked.

"Um, sorry, it's Grant."

"Nice to meet you. Live around here?"

"Um, yes, two blocks in that direction." He pointed, momentarily forgetting the sweat stains under his armpits. He quickly dropped his arm, hoping Ethan hadn't noticed.

Ethan cocked his head left. "I live a little further that way."

Grant expected they'd now part ways, but Ethan asked, "Where'd you come from?"

"What do you mean?" asked Grant.

"I mean, are you coming from the city?"

"No. My parents' restaurant."

"Where's that?"

"161st Street."

"I just moved here. Don't know where anything is."

"It's not too far from the Bronx courthouse."

"Don't know where that's either."

Of course not, you idiot. He just moved here, thought Grant.

"How 'bout you? Where'd you come from?" asked Grant, wanting to keep the conversation going.

"Me? Oh, I was, ah," he lowered his head, "I was visiting my mom at the hospital."

"I hope it's not serious," said Grant, thinking of his own mother who, as of late looked more tired than usual. But Grant didn't give him the chance to ask why his mom was hospitalized.

"Gotta run," Ethan said, preoccupied. He turned away and disappeared around the corner.

The next time Grant saw Ethan was on the first day of the

school year. He spotted him walking down the hallway, turning his head from left to right and looking at the sheet in his hands.

Grant's heart raced. Barely able to control his excitement, he hollered, "Ethan!"

Ethan's face lit up when he recognized Grant. "Hey. You go here too?" he asked.

"Yes, my first day. You a freshman too?"

"I am. My first class is homeroom, but I can't seem to find it."

"What's the room number?"

"322."

Grant smiled. "That's my homeroom too," he said, quietly thanking the school gods. They walked a couple of feet until they found the classroom. "Here it is," Grant said nervously.

"I would've found it sooner if you hadn't distracted me," Ethan joked.

Grant must have looked troubled because Ethan poked him in the ribs and said, "I was kidding. Come on, let's get inside before we're late."

From that day forward, they became inseparable, even though Ethan liked Home Economics and dragged Grant into enrolling in the class too, but he took pleasure in his new friend's love of cooking, and soon he too enjoyed it. At the restaurant, Grant's mom let them practice their cooking lessons and even shared some of her recipes with the boys. That year, Grant learned he had a talent for cooking.

As far back as Grant could remember, he was attracted to boys but had been too afraid to act on his feelings. Meeting Ethan brought those emotions to the surface. But it was not to be. Grant believed his best friend didn't share his attraction, so he hid his feelings from him, especially when Ethan talked about girls.

Theirs was the best friendship two boys ever had, and when it ended, Grant's world came crashing down on him.

———

"HE WAS YOUR CHILDHOOD FRIEND, wasn't he? A friend who committed suicide," Ramirez said. "Did you blame Wane Rudolph, Grant? Is that why you killed him?"

Grant shook his head and blinked away the tears. Finding his voice, he said, "No, no. I didn't kill anyone"

"But you blamed him for Ethan's death, didn't you?"

"No, why would I? I didn't even know he was Ethan's father."

"Yeah, you did, Grant. Wanna know how I know you killed Mr. Rudolph?" Ramirez didn't wait for an answer. He again flipped open the folder and took out a copy of the letter.

"This is Ethan Rudolph's suicide letter."

Grant looked confused. He weakly said, "Ethan didn't leave a letter."

"Yeah, he did. Didn't his mom tell you about it? She gave it to Father Sullivan and asked him to keep it in the archives."

"You're lying."

Ramirez shoved the letter in front of Grant. Is this Ethan's handwriting?"

Grant averted his eyes.

"Look at it," yelled Ramirez, causing Grant to jump.

He reluctantly looked down and recognized the familiar cursive writing. His eyes again filled with tears.

Ramirez snatched the letter away.

You might want to mention Rudolph's suspicion of same-gender attraction. That should get a rise out of him.

"Why do you suppose Mrs. Rudolph didn't tell you about the letter, Grant? Was it because Ethan wrote that his father thought you two were more than friends, breaking God's laws?"

Grant blurted, "What? No. We were just friends."

"I don't know, Grant, Ethan's father said you were his girlfriend."

"You're making that up."

"Would you like for me to read the letter to you?"

Grant's eyes went from staring at Ramirez to the letter. He swallowed, afraid to know what Ethan had written on his last day on Earth but needing to know.

"Well? Do you or don't you want to know what Ethan wrote?"

"Yes," he whispered.

Here we go. Read it slowly so every word sinks in.

Ramirez picked up the letter.

"Mom, I'm writing this letter to you because I don't want you to blame yourself for my death. You are a wonderful mom and I love you very much. But I cannot stand it when dad calls me names and pushes me around as if I'm a disappointment. I try to be obedient. My grades are good, and I go to church even though I hate it, so why does he call me a sissy and a fag? Dad accused me of having Grant for my girlfriend. That hurt me because I love Grant, but is dad right? Am I a sissy? I'm so confused, mom."

Ramirez paused and looked at Grant, whose tears were flowing faster than he could wipe them with his hands. "Did Mrs. Rudolph ever tell you Ethan loved you?"

Grant nodded and cleared his throat. His voice shook when he said," She said I was his best friend, but she never told me he left a note."

Ramirez continued reading.

"Grant is the only person I can talk to. He's my only friend. When I'm with him, I don't feel weak. Tell Grant he's the best friend I've ever had.

.   .   .

"STOP, PLEASE," pleaded Grant, who had stopped wiping away his tears.

Ramirez ignored him.

"You need to leave dad, mom. Even though you hide it from me, I know he hits you. I'm afraid he'll kill you someday, mom. He's already put you in the hospital."

Ramirez put down the letter and asked with concern in his voice, "Did he beat Ethan too, Grant?"

"Yes," he cried.

"Tell me about it."

"One day, Ethan didn't come to school for a couple of days. I got worried and went to see if he was all right. After his mom asked him if he wanted to see me, she let me in." Grant wiped his eyes. "Ethan said he had fallen when I saw his bruised face, but when I told him I didn't believe him, he confessed his father beat him."

"Didn't that make you mad?"

Delacroix clenched his jaw. "Yes, of course. It made me mad. That man was a monster."

"Anyone would be, Grant. That's understandable. Let me finish reading this."

Grant begged, "Please, I don't want to know the rest."

"Well, it's important you hear the rest, Grant." Ramirez again picked up the letter.

"I know you hate it when he puts you down, quoting those verses. He's so self-righteous. Thinks he's smarter than everyone. Perhaps he's insane. I hate him, and I don't want to hate my father, but I cannot go on living and taking his abuse. I hope when I'm gone, you'll leave him. You need to save yourself, mom. He believes everything it says in that book. I'm not strong, mom. Most days I find it hard to think. All I do is question myself and I'm tired of it. Please don't blame yourself and don't show this letter to dad. Forgive me for causing you pain, but I cannot live with a man who hates me. I love you. Ethan." Ramirez stowed the letter back into the folder.

"When you guys talked, did Ethan tell you how his father treated him?"

"That son of a bitch terrorized Ethan. "*Sissy boy,*" he spat out the words. "That's what he liked to call Ethan. The only time I saw Ethan happy was when he cooked with me and my mom at my parent's restaurant."

Time to wrap this up.

"Ethan died because of Wane Rudolph. That much is clear in that suicide letter. Isn't it true when you saw Mr. Rudolph at Coral Bells, he brought up all those sad memories you left behind in the Bronx?"

"Sure, I recognized him. I even got mad all over again, but I didn't kill him," Grant emphatically said.

"Oh no? Let me tell you how it all went down. When you saw Mr. Rudolph and he failed to recognize you, you got mad and plotted his death. You waited until that rain storm and showed up early to work, knowing the residents would still be asleep. You then let yourself into Rudolph's apartment and found him asleep wearing a CPAP mask. What a stroke of good luck that must have been. With those powerful hands of yours, you held him down and caused him to die of a heart attack."

Grant's legs bounced faster now. "No, no. I didn't kill him."

"You're going to continue to deny it? That mask left bruises on Mr. Rudolph's face, leading us to believe someone pressed down on it, someone strong like you. Ethan wrote he loved you. If it weren't for Rudolph, who knows if the friendship would have developed into something more? He was confused. In a normal household, he would've had the freedom to explore his feelings for you."

"Yes, all right?" he yelled. "It makes me mad. I hated that man. He robbed me of my future with my best friend." Grant was shaking now.

Lie to him about latex glove fingerprints.

"Grant, did you know we can recover fingerprints from latex gloves?" Iggy asked matter-of-factly.

"What?"

"Yeah. You should've taken those gloves with you. But that's not all we have. A witness saw you enter Mr. Rudolph's apartment. She heard you sneeze, Grant, and can describe you."

Grant's fear of prison exacerbated the shaking. He desperately needed that drink.

"Bet you thought you were alone in that corridor, but you forgot how loud you sneeze. That sneeze of yours prompted our witness to look through her door's peephole. Not only that, but Josephine Devin confirmed she let you in on the morning of Mr. Rudolph's death earlier than expected. Did you forget after you signed the timesheet she logged in the time? By the way, she remembered that sneeze of yours too."

I want a lawyer," Grant said, looking desperate.

"A lawyer will advise you to cooperate because juries look favorably on those who cooperate with police, but if you're willing to take a chance of having a longer prison sentence, then we can get you a lawyer. Your call."

Both Ramirez and Pierce held their breaths.

Grant looked like a trapped animal. Ramirez knew he had him.

"How did you get into the apartment, Grant? Did your friend Mace help you make a key during one of your card games?"

Pierce held his breath.

Delacroix visibly wilted.

"Mace carries around master keys for all the units," he murmured.

"Speak up," said Ramirez.

Delacroix gulped in a few breaths and said, "I befriended that slob, hanging out in his filthy workroom after work, playing cards and downing beers. We got to talking and he showed me a key-making kit he kept around as a hobby. I asked him to teach me how to use it. After a few weeks, I spiked his beer and slipped the master key from his chain when he fell asleep. I copied the key and clipped the master back onto his chain. It was easy."

"Tell me what happened on the morning you entered Mr. Rudolph's apartment."

Grant again lowered his voice. "I let myself in and found him attached to a machine with a mask on his face."

Ramirez leaned forward not wanting to tell Grant to speak up again lest he clam up now that they had him on the hook.

"I had never seen such a machine, but I figured it was to help him breathe. In the bathroom, I grabbed a towel, then went back into the bedroom and flipped the control switches on the machine to what I figured was the highest level. He thrashed about and, as you said, I held him down until he died. I took off the mask and wiped his face and neck and put the mask back on his face, turning him on the side the way I found him, and I left."

"You left the door unlocked, Grant. What did you do with the key?"

"I meant to throw it away, but I think it's still in the pocket of my slicker."

Ramírez rose. "Mr. Delacroix, I'm placing you under arrest for the murder of Wane Rudolph. Get up, turn around and put your hands behind your back.

Great job, Iggy.

Pierce took off his earpiece when Ramirez cuffed Delacroix and recited the Miranda Warning.

22

The news of the charismatic chef's arrest made the evening news. A shockwave spread throughout the building. It was all everyone talked about late into the evening.

Grace Johnson made her rounds like a politician feeding the residents of Coral Bells her version of the murder, playing her part as the mayor to the hilt.

"I've always been suspicious of him," she said to her listeners. "After all, why did a chef who worked at a famous restaurant in New York City come to work at an adult living facility and not some fancy restaurant or hotel? And he didn't even go to a big city like Philadelphia. No. He came to the Poconos because everyone knows we're the culinary capital of the world," she sarcastically said. "Ask yourselves, was he running from something? Mr. Rudolph didn't deserve to be killed in his sleep. Nobody deserves that." People agreed.

But in true Grace Johnson fashion, tempered her rhetoric with sympathy for the perpetrator. "But let's give Chef Delacroix the benefit of the doubt. He is an excellent chef, whom we all know and love. And let's not forget what a nasty individual Wane could be, not that he deserved to be murdered, but we don't know the entire story." After saying her piece, she'd walk away to find her next audience, leaving her *constituents* baffled.

Mace Leyton felt let down. He had enjoyed those evenings when the chef would sit with him for a game of cards and a beer. Sometimes he'd bring leftover appetizers. That he killed Wane Rudolph, a man who couldn't shut up about the bible, didn't bother Mace as much as losing a friend.

Jamie Alinsky held an emergency prayer meeting for the tragedy that had befallen the late Wane Rudolph. All members attended. At the end of the meeting, Alinsky informed everyone bible studies would continue once a week. No one objected.

Monica now believed Mr. Howard Martal had been under-cover. Her emotions ran the gamut from feeling proud to have been a small part of his investigation to surprise the chef killed Mr. Rudolph, to being glad he got arrested. After the detectives took the chef away, Monica couldn't sit still and called Josephine Devin, pulling her out of a deep sleep.

As soon as the barely awake security guard answered the telephone, Monica blurted she had to talk to someone and couldn't leave her post to join the others in the sitting room.

"Slow down. What the hell happened?"

"Sorry I woke you, Jo. Wane Rudolph did not die of a heart attack. I mean, he did die of a heart attack, but the chef caused it."

Josephine's drowsy head cleared. "Shit."

"It's all over the news. Everyone's gathered around the TV. Turn on the news, Jo."

Josephine said, "Hold on," and ran to her tv set. She tuned into BRCTV13, the local news channel. A commercial was running. She picked up the phone. "Monica, tell me what happened quickly before the commercials are done."

Monica described how she had many conversations with Mr. Martal or whatever his real name was. Josephine felt a tinge of jealousy that he hadn't spoken to her, not realizing she had given Frank Irizarry important information that helped Pierce solve the case.

BREAKING NEWS appeared on the screen.

"I gotta go, Monica. Thanks for calling me."

That evening, local reporters swarmed the residence with their camera crews and microphones. They interviewed people who had nothing bad to say about either Rudolph or the chef. The animosity felt by the bible studies group for Rudolph did not prevent them from saying nice things about him. As for the chef, everyone agreed on what an excellent cook he was. No one had an unkind word to say. Everyone was in disbelief because their beloved chef had murdered their dear neighbor, Mr. Rudolph.

No one except Grace Johnson, who was in her element. Giving the best performance of her life, she told the world how she suspected an investigation was underway when a stranger came asking questions. She told them how Rudolph broke up the bible studies class, implying not everyone liked him. And how she was not surprised the chef had killed him since everyone is capable of murder. By the time reporters interviewed her, she had the story down pat after having spread it around the building. Reporters left the premises, delighted they finally had a juicy story to tell.

The residents couldn't get enough of the news. Some moved away from the TV only to eat or take bathroom breaks, not wanting to miss anything new.

Jenaro Miller heard the news before it hit the airwaves. Pierce called him as soon as the police charged Delacroix, explaining in great detail the history Rudolph and Delacroix had shared. Miller had a lot of questions that Pierce patiently answered. He spent the rest of the day in isolation, trying to understand Wane, his friend who had caused his only son's death. He tearfully followed the story like everyone else on television.

When she heard the news, Guadalupe Garcia called her dear friend, Jenaro, offering to bring over a pot of coffee and a freshly baked pie. Miller kindly turned her down, promising to meet her for breakfast.

After hanging up with Mr. Miller, Pierce telephoned Frank Irizarry. Frank's ability to get the information he needed impressed Pierce. He saw in him the potential to become an excellent investigator. Reviewing his background, Pierce saw he tried to join the police force a few times. That kind of perseverance needed to be rewarded, and while he couldn't offer Frank a police officer's job, working at a private investigations agency, sometimes in liaison with the police, is the next best thing he could offer. *Besides*, Pierce thought, *I could use the help.*

Frank answered the phone with his usual enthusiasm.

"Mr. Pierce, so happy you called. We did it, didn't we?"

"We sure did, Frank. Couldn't have done it without you."

Hearing those words, he felt proud to have gained the respect of a true homicide detective.

"Thank you. Like I told you before, if you need anything, call me."

"I can do better than that, Frank. How'd you like to come work for me?"

Frank momentarily lost his voice.

Pierce said, "You there, Frank?"

"Ye, ye, yes, sir," Frank stammered.

"Well, what do you say?"

"Do you mean help you with homicide investigations?"

"As a private investigator, I don't get to solve homicide cases, Frank. The Rudolph case was a favor. My job is mainly providing evidence in matters such as divorce and infidelity investigations, child custody disputes, finding missing loved ones, serving legal papers, and a host of other things. You get the idea."

"I see," said Frank. "But it is possible your friend might want you to help solve another murder, right?"

Pierce laughed. He also hoped Iggy would send another homicide investigation his way. "Not likely, but you never know," he said. "I could use your help, Frank. What do you say?"

Frank thought he could learn a lot from a former homicide detective, even if he didn't get the chance to help him in a murder investigation again. It might be exciting and certainly more interesting than sitting around waiting for something interesting to happen at Coral Bells.

"Yes," Mr. Pierce. "I would be happy to work for you."

"Splendid. Come by my office tomorrow afternoon before your shift and we'll discuss the specifics of your employment."

"I will. Thank you again."

"See you tomorrow."

Pierce smiled. *Gotta love the guy.*

———

AFTER THE ARREST, a search of Grant Delacroix's premises turned up the missing key to Mr. Rudolph's apartment in the pocket of his raincoat. This piece of evidence further buttoned up the case against the chef.

Former Detective Howard Pierce, private investigator for Bloodhound Investigations, felt exhausted but fulfilled.

When he entered his old haunt to the cheers of his former team, he smiled with renewed energy. They had gathered at their favorite cop bar to celebrate. Ramirez raised his glass. "Here's to the best detective this unit ever had, Sergeant Howard Pierce." Everyone cheered.

When they quieted down, Pierce raised his glass. He toasted his former second-in-command. "Here's to Sergeant Ignacio Ramirez, the best second I could have ever wished for."

Ramirez, who was sitting next to Pierce, said, "If it weren't for you, Sarge, I wouldn't have given this case a second look. Thank you. You truly are a bloodhound."

The drinks kept coming. When the taxi dropped him off at home, not even his intoxicated mind could blur the joy he felt.

Howard Pierce once again felt like a homicide detective.

ACKNOWLEDGMENTS

It's been a little over two years since I introduced Howard Pierce in my detective novel, Simply Gregg. During that time, I've been developing this sequel—Bloodhound Investigations, slowly bringing my characters to life, and seeing them as real people in my imagination. In giving another case to my protagonist, Howard Pierce, I had to follow him through every step of the investigation, putting myself in his shoes as it were. The cameo appearances of a few of Howard's former colleagues from Simply Gregg were fun to include in this story. Although I spent countless hours writing and rewriting, doing research, and editing, editing, editing, I found the hard work was worth it when I finally finished it. I hope you will agree.

Thank you to my family and friends who continue to support my writing, and also to the people I do not know but have left positive reviews on social media for my work. I value your critique whether good or not so good. Honest feedback is what keeps me going. A special thank you to The Lady Writers of the Poconos for not only being my friends but for continuing to encourage me and my efforts to keep improving my story-telling abilities. To my brilliant cover designer, Wesley Goulart, what can I say? except thank you for your patience and always knowing what I want better than I can describe it.

If you enjoyed Bloodhound Investigations, please recommend it to your friends and family, and leave a review on

Amazon.com. It doesn't have to be long. 'I liked it,' works. Little-known authors need all the support and encouragement we can get to get our books noticed. I would appreciate your support.

Stay tuned to my next Howard Pierce novel, Book 3. I'm already meshing it out in my head. Hopefully, I will be able to publish it sooner than two years.

If you are suffering from depression and have nowhere to turn, know there are people who care and will help you. Please call the Suicide Prevention Hotline at 988. Your life is precious.

ABOUT THE AUTHOR

Evelyn Infante is a small business owner in the beautiful Pocono Mountains of Pennsylvania. Although writing for most of her life, she published her first novel in 2021, *Simply Gregg*—a story about a homicide detective, Howard Pierce, tasked with solving a difficult case months before retirement. This novel earned her the Fofky's Readers' Choice Award for Best Eclectic Book.

In *Bloodhound Investigations,* the sequel to *Simply Gregg,* Howard Pierce, now a private investigator, is hired to look into a citizen's suspicion that his friend did not die of natural causes. As in *Simply Gregg,* a case for homicide is going to be tough to prove, but this author, like her favorite PI, certainly loves a challenge.

Follow Evelyn Infante's latest Howard Pierce undertaking as her favorite fictional detective uncovers clues while tying together the puzzle pieces to solve yet another complex homicide.

www.ingramcontent.com/pod-product-compliance
Lightning Source LLC
Chambersburg PA
CBHW051506170626
46811CB00002B/682